THE HIGH COUNTRY YANKEE

Joel Garretson quit his job as Chief of Scouts to travel to Texas and claim his piece of land. He needed to forget the killings he had seen — and done — fighting the Sioux and the Crow in Montana . . . But he soon has to confront Texas *pistoleros* and then, aided by a bunch of ex-Missouri brush boys, he faces the task of rescuing two women held by *comancheros* in their stronghold . . . In the territory of the Llana Estacado, New Mexico, the violent blood-letting will commence . . .

ELLIOT CONWAY

THE HIGH COUNTRY YANKEE

Complete and Unabridged

LINFORD
Leicester

First published in Great Britain in 2005 by
Robert Hale Limited
London

First Linford Edition
published 2006
by arrangement with
Robert Hale Limited
London

The moral right of the author has been asserted

British Library CIP Data

Conway, Elliot
    The high country Yankee.—Large print ed.—
Linford western library
    1. Western stories
    2. Large type books
    I. Title
    823.9'14 [F]

    ISBN 1–84617–280–2

Published by
F. A. Thorpe (Publishing)
Anstey, Leicestershire

Set by Words & Graphics Ltd.
Anstey, Leicestershire
Printed and bound in Great Britain by
T. J. International Ltd., Padstow, Cornwall

This book is printed on acid-free paper

In memory of Tex Larrigan
(Irene Ord), a B.H.W. writer and
long-time amigo

1

The tall, gaunt-faced rider swung down from an equally tall, rangy-boned horse. He stood for several minutes eyeing the scene across what, he reckoned in the wet season, if they had rain in this goddamned corner of Texas, would be a fair-sized creek. Now it was only a stretch of caked mud-holes holding an inch or two of bad-smelling water a thirsty dog would be reluctant to drink.

He could see the remains of the shack, a stone chimney breast and part of one still standing, sun-bleached planked side wall. What had once been the roof was lying shattered on the ground, and only knee-deep grass grew on the vegetable patch.

Sighing deeply he turned and looked his horse in the face and without any rancour in his voice, he said, 'Crowbait, if I was a man who always looked on the black side of things, I would say that we've hauled our asses all the way down Mr Goodnight's cattle trail just for the exercise. For if you cast your beady-eyes across that hog wallow of a crick you'll see the property that belongs to one, Mr Joel Garretson — that's me — bequeathed to the aforementioned character by his late uncle Jeremiah Garretson.'

Crowbait's top lip curled back baring yellow tombstone teeth in a snorting snarl.

'Yeah, well that's m'be your opinion of the situation, but that's what was writ in that letter handed to me back there at the fort. And before you show your displeasure again, the location is right accordin' to my readin' of the map that lawyer fella sent me. Though I'll admit I've seen more homely-lookin' shacks after Chief Gall's bare-assed hair-lifters have paid them a visit.

'But it ain't put a sore look on my face, Crowbait. We're alive, ain't we? More than 'Long-hair' Custer and his poor troopers are when we saw them all shot to hell up on those ridges along the Greasy Grass.' Joel's face stoned over as he relived the fearful sight that greeted the column coming up from the Rosebud. He would have been lying alongside them if he hadn't taken a Crow buck's arrow in his right arm while scouting for General 'Bearcoat' Miles two days before Custer and his 7th Cavalry rode out to knock seven kinds of hell out of the Sioux.

Joel reached out and patted Crowbait's flank. 'I ain't forgettin' you stopped a coupla feathered sticks yourself, pard. But you kept goin' and out rode those half starved apologies of horses the Injuns favour until I could get my back against a big rock and hold off the red heathens with the big Sharps until General Miles himself at the head of a full regiment rode by and saved me from gettin' an Injun haircut.'

'So here we are, in Texas, and without a roof above our heads, though that ain't anything unusual. But bein' I ain't as young as I was, I had a hankerin' to lie in a real bed, sleep with my pants and boots off. Havin' not to worry about gettin' jumped by the Sioux and the Crow. It ain't much to hope for, Crowbait, for a man who's been bullet and arrow shot in the service of the Union.'

Joel climbed back on to his saddle again and, picking up the reins, pulled Crowbait's head round to head back to Little Springs and to think of a way a middle-aged, ex-chief of General Miles's scouts, a long ways from his friends, could earn a living. Cow-herding? Joel let out a guffaw of a laugh that had Crowbait's ears jerk up.

He certainly hadn't enough cash to rebuild his property, even if he could make it as a sodbuster. And as for trying to sell his holding he had no idea of the price he could ask, or knew anyone crazy enough to want to buy it. Joel opined he would have to live on chewed grass as Crowbait did. Joel's lips hardened in twin stubborn lines.

And by hell, he thought, he would do that rather than scout for General Miles again.

Joel had discovered he was a Texas landowner at Fort Ellis, Montana. He had left the burial details on the Greasy Grass to escort Major Reno and Captain Benteen's wounded troopers back to the army's base on the Yellowstone. They were all that was left of Colonel Custer's command. He then had ridden, non-stop to Fort Ellis, General Sheridan's HQ. He had stormed in on the army commander as he was discussing with his staff the next moves against the Sioux after the army's fearful and bloody setback.

'General!' he had burst out. 'I've seen enough dead men, some of them bluecoat and red skinned, I was proud to call my friends back there along the Little Big Horn to haunt me the rest of my life. I'm quittin' bein' an army scout.' He glowered at Sheridan and his staff and the pain from his arm wound wasn't making him any calmer. 'The army don't need scouts any more. Every hostile and their kin along the Big Horn will be high-tailin' for Canada!' He then banged shut the office door before Sheridan could call the guard and have him thrown in the stockade. As he was watering and feeding Crowbait prior to leaving the fort, with no idea in which direction he was about to head in, the post corporal handed him a large envelope, sealed with red wax.

On opening the packet he read the officially worded letter which was pinned to another sheet of paper, also stamped with seals. He read the letter and discovered he was now a land-owner, though his piece of real estate was several weeks trailing south, in Texas, close by a river called the Brazos. The ride, Joel thought, would take his mind off the dead along the Big Horn.

In no time at all he had Crowbait loaded up with several days' supplies, after he had checked that his mount's wounds were healed up enough to bear the extra weight and the rigours of the trail. The easiest way to Texas, Joel opined, was to cross over into Wyoming and pick up the main cattle trail. A regular turnpike he had been led to believe, chewed out by the longhorns' hoofs being driven up from Texas.

He was just about ready to ride out when the colour-sergeant ran up to him and handed him a small box wrapped in waxed paper. 'The general sent you these, Joel,' the sergeant said. 'A box of his finest ceegars. It's all over the post that you're goin' to take up bein' a sodbuster in Texas.' The sergeant grinned. 'And according to old Phil, ceegars in Texas are rolled outa dried longhorn droppin's.'

Joel grinned. 'And by hell the old warhorse was right.' He had promised himself he would save at least one of the general's cigars to smoke in his first permanent home since he had been britched, but he had smoked them all long before Crowbait had shaken the dust of New Mexico from his hoofs.

He had stopped at Little Springs, the town the lawyer had mentioned being close to his land to buy supplies, and ask to be directed to his holding. The youth wearing a deputy marshal's badge had said that he should take the west trail out of town and once he hit the Brazos follow it south until he came to the first creek leading into the river. 'Your land, mister,' the young deputy had said, 'is just across the crick. Though I oughta tell you there ain't been anyone livin' on it for years so there ain't much of the place still standing.'

Thanking the lawman for his help, Joel rode out of Little Springs on the last few miles of the long, ball-aching journey for him and Crowbait with his high hopes somewhat dampened by the deputy's worrying news about his place being run down. As well as purchasing supplies Joel had bought a handful of dark-brown thin cheroots having the smell of a not too clean livery barn about them. He had lit one when he had reached the Brazos and they tasted as bad as they smelt, the acrid smoke causing Crowbait to snort and roll his red-rimmed eyes in protest.

'Crowbait,' he said. 'Old Bearcoat was right: Texas ceegars ain't rolled outa tobacco. You're durn fortunate you ain't got one stuck between your teeth.'

When he first caught sight of his property Joel was glad he had smoked all his Havanas. He was too put out at what he was gazing at to appreciate a fine smoke.

2

Marshal Bill Tweedy walking along Main Street in his usual left-legged swinging gait to his office to relieve Deputy Slatts saw the lone rider coming into town by way of the east trail. By his deputy's description the marshal figured the stranger was the man he had told him about. Sounded like a Yankee, the kid had also told him, and had asked for directions to old Jeremiah Garretson's piece of dirt.

The marshal gave a twitching smirk of a smile as he thought of what the Yankee, who had trailed here from God knows where, would be feeling on clapping his eyes on his farm, land old man Garretson hadn't lived on since the end of the war. Though the war had been fought and lost ten odd years ago, Tweedy still hated the Yankees. The only time he had crossed the Mason-Dixon line was as a sergeant in General Hood's Texas division to take part in the bloody slaughterhouse of the Battle of Gettysburg. He had been one of the lucky Johnny Rebs only ending up with a busted knee. A hell of a lot of young Texas men who had marched through the cornfields with drums beating, flags waving, hollering how they were going to sweep the blue-bellies off Cemetery Ridge, were still up there, buried in Yankee soil.

The pain in his knee, like his hatred for the Union, was still with him. 'I'm Marshal Tweedy,' he said, as the rider drew up alongside him. 'I take it you're the Yankee who spoke to my deputy this morning, the new owner of the Garretson farm.' Farm! The marshal had to fight hard to hold back his laughter. It would take a whole army of field hands to get that land ready for planting and rebuild the shack. Then he did some quick assaying of the Yankee.

He was an *hombre* with a cold-eyed

11

stare that went right through him, as tall as he was but not so beefy. He favoured a long hide coat and a wide, droopy-brimmed plains hat. By the length of the pistol sticking out of the top of his pants it looked to be .44 Walker Colt, a stopping-dead-in-the-tracks weapon. As well as the booted Winchester, Marshal Tweedy noticed the blue-tinged metal barrel of a heavy calibre long gun protruding out of his bedroll.

To complete his arsenal, the Yankee had a big bladed knife sheathed on his right hip. All in all, the marshal had to admit, he looked like a man ready and capable of facing any trouble coming his way. How he earned his living he couldn't rightly guess, but he knew the tall man hadn't a drop of sodbuster's blood in his veins. His horse, though no two-year-old, was as lean and fit and as leery-eyed as its rider.

Joel reckoned that the stiffness in the marshal's leg was an old war wound. He had no doubts by the curl-lipped scowls the fat-gutted lawman was giving him that he wasn't too fond of Yankees. He cursed under his breath. He had hard-assed it to Texas to get out of reach of unfriendly Indians only to be met by not so friendly white-eyes.

'Yeah, that's me, Marshal, Joel Garretson.' Joel kept the anger out of his voice. He gave a thin-lipped smile. 'I've seen what the lawyer fella wrote was left to me by my uncle, Marshal, and it sure ain't home sweet home, even for an old mountain man like me. It ain't worth the trip from Montana. M'be I could sell the land.'

'If that's what you have in mind, Yankee,' the marshal said, 'the man you want to talk to is Ben McDowell, boss of the Slash Y. He's been runnin' cattle over that land of yours for nigh on eight years. He figures it's his land by default of the owner, your kinsman, not workin' his land. But that's something you'll have to take up with a lawyer. The only problem you've got there is that the nearest shyster is up at the state capital a coupla days' ride north of here.' This time the marshal showed his one-in-the-eye-for-you-Yankee smile. 'Though I reckon his fee will be a damn sight more than you'll get for the land. There ain't much call for ploughin' land, bein' this is cattle country.'

Keeping his face straight, Joel said, 'Well m'be I'll hang on to my land, Marshal, and raise woollies. A Yankee sheepman oughta liven things up more than somewhat in longhorn territory.'

Joel kneed Crowbait into a trot, leaving behind him a red-faced, word-less, spluttering lawman.

He dismounted outside the livery barn and asked the owner, a grey, grizzled old man, to water and feed Crowbait. He flicked a silver dollar into the eager grasping hands of a young boy whom he took to be the barn owner's helper, and told him to give Crowbait a good brush before bedding him down. Crowbait, Joel thought, deserved a bit of fussing over, the first since leaving Fort Ellis. The boy's grin split his face. 'I'll brush him till his coat shines, mister, or so help me, you can take back your dollar.'

Now it was time he was being fussed over, like finding a room and a bed until he sorted out what he was going to do with his land. And to sit down to home-cooked meals at a table. Too many meals of warmed-up beans and fatty sowbelly played hell with a man's guts. The barkeep in the saloon across the street would be bound to know where what he craved for was available. The town marshal, he knew, would be reluctant to give him the time of day.

The only other customer in the saloon was the young kid deputy tucking into a big steak as though eating was going out of fashion. Though the kid had manners enough to stop his chewing long enough for him to ask if he had found his property OK.

'I did, Deputy,' Joel replied. 'And as you so rightly pointed out to me the shack will need a whole heap of work done to it before I can move in. But that ain't the problem right now, boy. I'm seekin' a room and board for a few days until I sort myself out. I didn't want to ask your boss because he's made no secret of the fact he don't take a shine to Yankees.'

'You can stay with me and my ma,' Deputy Slatts said, without any hesitation. 'We've got a spare room and Ma's a good cook. And she could do with the extra cash, being my pa's dead.'

'That would suit me fine, boy, if it's OK with your ma,' Joel said. 'And as long as the marshal don't bawl you out for doin' a goddamned Yankee a charitable act.'

Deputy Slatts grinned. 'Don't take any heed of that old sourpuss, mister. He's hated you Yankees ever since one of you put a minie ball through his knee at someplace in Pennsylvania during the war. He won't give me any grief because he knows he'll get no one else to act as his deputy on the pay he gives me.' He reached out his hand. 'I'm Jim

Slatts,' he added.

Joel gripped the offered hand in a firm handshake. 'Garretson, Joel Garretson.' He smiled. 'A true-blood Yankee hailin' from Montana.' Raising his voice, he called over to the barkeep. 'Mister, I'd be obliged if you'd fix me up with a plate of what the deputy marshal here is enjoyin', and a coupla beers.'

Before the barkeep could see to Joel's order, a series of gunshots rang out from the head of Main Street.

'Jesus Christ!' gasped Jim Slatts, knocking the table sideways with his knees as he sprang to his feet. 'It sounds like the marshal's in trouble!' All thumbs, he began to buckle on his gunbelt that had been draped over the back of his chair, cursing as he did so.

Joel saw the strained whiteness of the young deputy's farmboy-looking face. He glimpsed the sheen of fear in the boy's eyes and being that he had taken a shine to him, hoped the trouble he had heard wasn't too serious because the deputy didn't have the cut of a man who could use his pistol with great effect in a tight situation.

Jim smashed the bar doors back against the saloon walls as he burst through them and Joel heard the pounding of his feet as he sped along the boardwalk in the direction of the shooting. The boy might be as scared as hell, Joel opined, but he wasn't chickening out of his responsibilities. Though showing grit wouldn't prevent him from getting himself shot. A whole heap of brave men had got themselves killed along the Greasy Grass.

Joel gave the barkeep a quizzical look as he came across the room to the door to see for himself what the shooting was all about.

'Do you get much shootin' here, mister?' he asked.

The barkeep shook his head. 'The only shootin' we get in town is when some drunken ranch-hand on pay night wings himself or his pard when tryin' out some *pistolero* fancy fast draw tricks.'

The barkeep stepped out on to his porch then quickly ducked back inside at the sound of more gunfire along the street.

'The shootin's for real, mister!' the barkeep blurted out. 'There's two guns firin' from Benson's store front window at the kid hunkered down behind some crates opposite. And it looks like the marshal has stopped a bad one; he's stretched out on his back in the middle of the street.'

'What the hell's in a store that warrants two gunmen to shoot down a lawman in his own town?' asked Joel, again puzzle-eyed. 'Gold-wrapped candy bars for Chris' sake? Ain't you gotta bank in Little Springs to rob?'

'No we ain't,' the barkeep said. 'All I know is that Deputy Slatts will end up like the marshal if he don't get any help.' He leaned over his bar and lifted a battered stock, single-barrelled shotgun from a shelf. He broke it open to check the load then snapped it shut with a loud grate of a click. He smiled weakly at Joel. 'The deputy is my wife's favourite nephew. She'll use this gun on me if she knew I was still servin' beer when the kid was gettin' shot at.'

'Those fellas in the store are in a killin' mood,' Joel said. 'And if they've got long guns they'll pick you off before you get within shootin' range of that heirloom you're holdin'.'

'That pleasant thought had already crossed my mind,' the barkeep growled. 'But the kid . . . '

'You stay put,' Joel said. 'I'll go and even up the odds in the kid's favour. He's too well-mannered a boy to be shot down like a dog.'

'There ain't but a half-dozen men in town,' the barkeep said. 'But I could round them up and ring those two bastards in.'

'In the meantime the kid could get himself shot,' replied Joel. 'And how is Mr Benson farin' if he's still in his store? And the marshal could only be winged. This business needs settlin' quickly for all concerned. Did you see their horses in front of the store?'

The barkeep shook his head. 'Apart from the marshal lyin' there, the street's deserted.'

'That means the sonsuvbitches' mounts are tied up at the back,' Joel said. 'They've made their first mistake.'

He gave a fierce all-tooth grin that sent cold shivers down the barkeep's spine. He had only met the horse-faced Yankee a few minutes ago, yet he confidently tagged him as a manhunter or an Indian fighter. A breed of men who no longer operated in this part of Texas but plied their killing trade in the lawless badlands west of the Pecos where it was said even God had washed his hands of ever bringing sweetness and kindness to the men, white, brown and red, who roamed that territory.

The barkeep smiled for the first time since he had heard the shooting. 'You intend usin' the bastards' horses to draw them out into the open, mister?'

'That I do, barkeep,' Joel replied. 'That I do. Then they'll make another mistake — their last — by fireballin' out of the store to chase after their spooked horses.'

'Ain't you goin' to take your Winchester, mister?' the barkeep said, as Joel made for the door.

Joel turned and gave his death's head grin again. 'I've got a gun with my gear at the livery barn that's a mite more suitable in this two-to-one kinda situation.'

And the barkeep wondered if the tall Yankee was talking about a Gatling gun.

★   ★   ★

Boyd, a mean-faced man, dirty-mouthed his cousin, Gus, for landing them in one helluva stinking creek. It would have been wiser to have gone hungry for a few more days and made it to New Mexico where the law had no flyers posted on them than to have ridden into this dog dirt town stirring up more trouble for themselves.

There was already a price on their heads of $1000 dead or alive for several counts of murder and stage and bank robberies, and if that big-gutted gimp of a marshal lying out there was dead, then the ante on their heads would go sky-high. Boyd licked fear-dried lips. It could sic the Texas Rangers on them and those wild boys followed a trail as doggedly as an Indian and dealt out swift justice with the gun or the hanging rope.

Their misfortunes had begun in a whorehouse in another dump of a town fifty miles east of here. Gus, feeling the urge for a woman, suggested stopping off there to have a drink or two and have some fun with a couple of short-time girls. Fun! Boyd spat on the floorboards. If having a posse's bullets whizzing past your ears while trying to pull up your pants on the run was fun, then by hell they had a whole load of fun.

They were just raising a sweat with

two big-breasted whores when there came a hammering at the room door that stopped their performance in mid-thrust. Then came the yell of, 'It's the law! You two Murphys come out with your hands grabbin' air, or we'll come in shootin'! Now you wouldn't want those fine gals you're humpin' hurt, would you, boys?'

One thing Boyd always saw eye to eye with Gus was that neither of them gave a hoot who got hurt as long as it wasn't them. Grabbing their gunbelts, practically bare-assed, they flung themselves through the window and on to the balcony, dropping down into the street and jumping in the saddles of two of the posse's horses, riding low over the horses' necks like Indians to escape the hot lead cutting through the air all around them.

But the 'fun' hadn't ended. That came when they felt safe enough from pursuit to draw up their stolen mounts to a gentle canter and Gus told him that the small wad of dollar bills, their only cash, had dropped out of his pants pocket somewhere along the route of their mad dash from the cat-house room. Now they hadn't a red cent to buy supplies or feed for the horses until they could pull off a heist in New Mexico, territory they were not familiar with. And that son-of-a-bitch, Gus, only grinned at him and said, 'We'll just have to rob us a bank, Boyd.'

'You'll have to build one first,' he had replied, with a drop-dead glare. 'Between here and the New Mexican border there ain't anyone but widow women to rob safely. And don't even think of liftin' a few cows from a rancher, that's the surest way of gettin' our necks stretched. We'll just have to go hungry after all.'

'There ain't no need for us to go hungry,' Gus said. 'We're ridin' in the direction of a town of sorts. There'll have to be a store there. We can at least get us some rations.'

'We ain't got to forget,' Boyd said, 'that there's a bunch of lawmen behind us. We could be losin' more than our cash the next time they catch up with us.'

Gus grinned. 'One sight of two hard-eyed *pistoleros* and the store-keeper will keel over like some old maid comin' face to face with a breech-clouted buck with lust in his eyes. It ain't like robbin' a bank. We'll be in and out of that town faster than you can spit.'

Boyd spat again and growled to himself. And that was the last joke Gus made. Having half his ear blown off didn't put a man in a humorous frame of mind.

The old goat of a storekeeper didn't go jelly-legged when they burst into the store with pistols fisted. The son-of-a-bitch called them two no-good, mangy saddle-bums, and grabbing a big pistol, cut loose at them, shredding Gus's left ear. Gus howled like a kicked dog and, naturally, as mad as hell with pain, shot the the storekeeper well and truly dead.

Then things got worse. Now there

was a law-badge man lying out there in the dirt and another one pulling shots at them from across the street. Robbing a bank would have been easier.

Boyd was thinking it was time they called it a day and cut and run for it before some citizens turned out to back up the lawman. And he had to be dealt with before they dashed out for their horses, or it was risking being shot in the back if the bastard had a long gun.

During the lull in the firing, Boyd heard Gus call out, 'I think some of the sonsuvbitches are out back, I heard our horses movin' around out there.'

Boyd did some more cursing. If the horses were gone and they could get out of this trap in one piece they would have to hoof it all the way to the border. He suddenly had a pressing urge to blow off Gus's other ear. 'Let's get to hell outa here,' he said. 'But carefully.'

Boyd and Gus peered cautiously out of the back door of the store. It was as they had feared, their horses were gone.

'The gunfire could have spooked

them, Boyd,' Gus said.

Boyd stuck his head further out of the doorway. 'Well, they ain't spooked far,' he said. 'The pair of them are standin' near that patch of brush.'

'I see 'em,' Gus replied. 'We've been worryin' for nothin'.'

'Have we?' said Boyd, still casting suspicious-eyed glances around. He was damn sure he had tied his mount securely to a back porch post. Yet he could see no signs of anyone who could have loosened the reins and it was open ground right up to the stretch of bush 450, 500 yards away, well out of accurate Winchester range.

'We step out nice and easy, Gus,' he said, 'ready for trouble, something don't smell right. There could be men lurkin' on both sides of the store waitin' for us to show ourselves. If I'm worrin' for nothin' then you go and get the horses. I'll stay and cover this door just in case that bastard across the street, bein' that he's wearin a badge, thinks he oughta come in hot pursuit of us.'

Joel took a deep breath as he waited for his hands to steady after his mad-ass dash to the line of brush. He had loosened the horses and set them off far enough to draw out the two gunmen. And then he had to do some haring of his own to the brush, an ideal ambush spot for a man with a long range buffalo gun.

Joel didn't believe in taking chances when it came to killing, like facing up to your enemy and fighting fair. The Indians he had fought had taught him many things, one being that you killed your enemy any sneaky way you could. Col Custer had taken a boldass chance and got him and his boys slaughtered.

He drew a bead through the back sights of the Sharps on the gunman nearest the back door. The Sharps was a single-shot weapon, but Joel had no doubt that he could reload before the partner of the man he was about to blow to hell and beyond made it back to the shelter of the store. He gently eased back the hammer.

Boyd staggered back several paces, hands grabbing at the air as though seeking support as the heavy slug struck him in the chest with the force of a swinging hammer blow. It ripped its bloody way through Boyd's body to embed itself deeply in the stout planking of the store wall. Boyd thudded on to the ground without hearing the shot that had killed him.

Gus, halfway to the horses, heard the bang of the gun. Alarmed he spun round and saw Boyd go down in a flurry of arms and legs. He had only a split-second of time to seek out the big-gun man when Joel's second shot ended his life as quickly and as painfully as his partner's demise.

Deputy Slatts got up from behind his barricade of crates, the two rifle shots still ringing in his ears. He couldn't tell how he had worked it out, but the way he was reasoning the two shots signified two dead gunmen. Then he began to think of who it was who had fired the shots. No one in town owned a rifle with a discharge sounding like a small cannon. It could have only been the Yankee stranger's doing. For some reason or other he had come to his aid. And thank Sweet Jesus for that, he added fervently.

Backing on his feelings about the way things had panned out, he ran the few paces to Marshal Tweedy's body, though just to be on the safe side he kept his gaze and gun on the store door. As he knelt down alongside the marshal he heard the old lawman groan, and gasped out a thankful prayer. 'He's still alive, Uncle Grover!' he called out to the barkeep, as he came running up to him. 'But he's bleeding badly; we've got to get him to the doc's pronto!'

Then he heard the Yankee shout out from the store, 'Hold your fire, Deputy! I'm comin' out! Them two fellas ain't about to do any more shootin' this side of the gates of Hell!'

Joel came out on to the porch, the Sharps held high across his chest, mountain-man fashion. He saw Deputy Slatts and his barkeep kinsman lifting up the body of the marshal.

'Is he still alive?' he asked. 'The storekeeper ain't, the bastards shot him dead.'

'Yeah, he's still breathing, Mr Garretson,' Jim replied, soberly. 'Though for how long will be up to what the doc can do for him. And thanks for backing me up. It wouldn't have been long before those two sonsuvbitches plugged me as well.'

'Yeah, that's what I reckoned,' Joel said, straight-faced. 'Then I would have had to look elsewhere for a rented room.'

Jim grinned at him, saying nothing but thinking that if the Yankee hadn't sided with him his ma could have had two rooms to rent.

Joel stepped down on to the street. 'Let me give you a hand, Deputy,' he said. He grinned at Jim. 'But don't tell the old Reb a goddamned blue-belly helped you to get him to the doc's or he'll lose the will to stay alive.'

3

Widow Jemima Slatts, if she hadn't been a founder member of the Little Springs Church Meeting society, would have cursed her son for bringing a perfect stranger to her house as a prospective lodger.

Yes, she had a room to spare; it had been rented to a spinster sister of the Reverend Barker, the circuit preacher, but she had left town to visit a sick relative across in New Mexico. But it wasn't vacant for a male lodger, a bewhiskered Yankee who smelt as though he hadn't bathed for weeks. And who didn't seem at ease living under a roof. He was spooning down the second bowl of mutton stew she had placed before him as though his eating was as irregular as his bathing habits.

Even in her wildest dreams Jemima had never thought she would have had a killer of two men sitting at her dining-table. Though to be fair, according to Jimmy's telling of the shooting, the Yankee tough had saved his life. And her Christian upbringing had taught her that evil deeds were to be forgiven and returned with good charitable acts. And she could do with the extra cash a lodger would bring in. What she earned cleaning and doing the washing for the town's doctor and Jimmy's pay as a deputy didn't leave much to spend on extras.

Now she had a further worry: Jimmy had told her the disturbing news that he had been asked by the mayor to take on the job of town marshal until Mr Tweedy was on his feet again. Up till now there had been no serious shooting trouble in Little Springs but ungodly men from below the Rio Grande and west from the Panhandle passed through the town. Seeing a young boy wearing a marshal's badge could be a tempting sight for the lawless breed.

Joel was enjoying the finest stew he had ever tasted. His regular stews' main ingredients had been the flesh of every four-legged creature that roamed in the high country, and sometimes, when the winters were long and hard, anything that wriggled or crawled. He glanced up at his landlady, not an uncomely woman he thought, and saw the down-the-nose look she was giving him as she placed a freshly brewed pot of coffee on the table and guessed that she wasn't overjoyed at having him as a paying guest.

He wasn't making it any pleasurable for her by eating with as many table manners as a hungry hog and smelling like a whole pen full of them. He laid down his spoon and got to his feet.

'I reckon a man would have to ride a long way to partake of a better-tastin' stew, ma'am,' he said, smiling. 'No wonder that boy of yours is well filled out. And it was him who talked me into applyin' for that spare room he said you've got, but it's your house, ma'am, and if I'm puttin' you out any by bein' here you just say so. I'll find myself another room, or a dry barn someplace.' His face hardened. 'I ain't hidin' the fact that I'm a rough man with rough ways. The trade I followed was a dangerous and desperate business. Not a trade for storekeepers or travellin' salesmen. I ain't some drifter or owlhoot on the run from the law. Any killin' I was forced to do was legal like.'

Jemima's face reddened, feeling ashamed of her unkindly thoughts about Mr Garretson. She couldn't meet his cold-eyed gaze as she spoke. 'You're welcome to the room, Mr Garretson!' she almost blurted out. 'I, I just didn't expect a . . . man.'

Joel smiled again. 'I'm a long ways from lookin' like a spinster lady, but I'll keep out of your way. I've got folk to see about the sellin' of my land. You'll only see me at mealtimes. Now it's time I washed some of this trail dust off me.'

'In the outhouse at the back there's a bath and a boiler with water in it, I use the place as a washhouse. The fire is still burning so the water should be hot enough for a bath. I'll go and check that it is while you sit down and digest your meal.'

★   ★   ★

Jemima, finishing off her household chores, gazed out of the kitchen window and saw her new lodger sitting, bare to the waist, stitching up a tear in his shirt. She smiled slightly. At least he should smell somewhat sweeter, she thought. Then, as if it was the natural thing to do, she stepped outside and walked across to him. Relaxed after his hot soaking and concentrating on his needlework, Joel didn't hear her approaching until she spoke.

'I'll do that for you, Mr Garretson,' Jemima said. 'It'll be no bother, I've some of Jimmy's clothes to mend. And any washing you want doing.' Her eyes widened in shock as she saw the white puckered scars of old wounds on his chest and back. Mr Garretson hadn't been lying when he had told her that the business he had been engaged in had been hazardous.

Joel sprang to his feet, his turn to be embarrassed. He covered up his chest with his shirt as though he was standing jaybird naked.

'Yeah, well, that's most obligin' of you, ma'am,' he stammered. 'You can see I ain't an expert with a needle and cotton.' Though in no way could he take up the widow's offer of doing his washing. His drawers were more holes and patches than drawers. He grinned weakly. 'It's time I bought myself some new gear. I intended to do just that when I got settled on my new property, but on seein' my place it kinda put the buyin' of clothes right outa my mind.'

Then, Joel thought, that now the widow seemed to be looking more favourably on him, he ought to repay her offer of darning his shirt with an offer of his own.

'While I'm here, ma'am,' he said,

'bein' your boy is now a full-time lawman, I'm willin' to do his chores about the place. Chop logs, mend fences, holes in the barn roof, whatever.'

Joel saw the look of concern and fear come into the widow's face at the mention of her lawman son.

'Your boy will be OK,' he said. 'It seems a quiet town and he shouldn't be forced to show his authority.'

'You were forced to kill two men in this *quiet* town, Mr Garretson,' Jemima replied, stone-faced.

There was no answer to that, Joel thought. Then he said, 'I'll keep an eye on the boy while I'm in town, ma'am.' He wondered why he had said that. He had enough to occupy his time trying to sort out what he was going to do with his property without playing nursemaid to a kid. Plus the fact that he had come to Texas to get away from a life of shooting and killing.

'Oh will you, Mr Garretson!' Jemima cried, the apprehension and fear lifting from her face as she smiled at him.

And that sweet smile made Joel realize the widow woman was more comely than his first opinion of her. He wasn't too old to still appreciate the blood stirring, lustful pleasure a genuine smile from a fine-looking female did to him.

Joel took a grip of himself. The smile wasn't the skin-deep inviting smile of a two-dollar whore but the showing of grateful thanks of a woman worried about her son's wellbeing. If the widow ever knew what had flittered through his mind about her, she would force him out of her house with a shotgun.

'Now I'll take that shirt, Mr Garretson,' Jemima said. 'I'll have it mended in no time at all.' She reached out and took the shirt from Joel's hand, not without some slight tugging on her part.

She smiled again. 'I'm a widow, have a grown-up son. I'm used to seeing men stripped to the waist.' Though, she added under her breath, none more battle scarred.

★ ★ ★

Fifteen minutes later, wearing a neatly darned shirt, Joel walked along the street to the livery barn to saddle up Crowbait and ride out to the Slash Y and see if he could persuade the owner, Mr McDowell, to buy his land off him. He would probably have to sell it at a rock-bottom price, but that ought to grubstake him to ride further west seeking employment. There was nothing for him here in Little Springs. Though, to be fair, he hadn't yet worked out what employment he was looking for. At least, Joel thought, he was well away from the mayhem and bloodshed along the Powder and Rosebud rivers.

Before leaving town he decided to pay a call on Marshal Slatts to see how the youngster was coping with being responsible for the upholding of the law

41

in Little Springs.

From her front porch Jemima watched the tall gaunt figure of her lodger walking along the board-walk, his long, well-worn coat scuffing the dust. She had briefly branded him a killer and the fearsome array of scars on his upper body spoke of probably many more killings Mr Garretson had carried out in that dangerous business he said he had been engaged in. Yet he had been as embarrassed as a young girl at showing his body to her. For some reason, she didn't know why, women's curiosity, she put it down to, Jemima wondered if Mr Garretson was married and had a family.

She smiled with relief as she saw him cross the street and head for the marshal's office. Though, she suddenly thought, she was putting a lot of hope and trust in a man she had only known for a few hours. And a damn Yankee at that.

Marshal Jimmy Slatts cursed loudly

in the confines of his office as the back flicked pistol missed its holster and dropped on to the floorboards with a resounding clatter. He had been practising a *pistolero*'s fast draw with little success. How the heck, he thought disappointedly, could he get the drop on two, maybe three, desperadoes if it took him so long to pull out his pistol?

'Speed ain't essential, Marshal,' a grinning Joel said from the door. 'Though that will come with practice.'

Jimmy's face reddened. 'Oh heck, I didn't think anyone was watchin' me.' Then added despondently, 'I'll never make a marshal. A gunman could kill me twice over before my pistol cleared leather.'

'As I told you, Marshal,' Joel said. 'Fast drawin' is overplayed. It ain't always true that a man who hits first hits hardest. More than often he'll miss with his first shot. A shooter who takes that extra second to aim true generally gets the edge.'

Joel hard-eyed Jimmy. 'If you have to

pull out your gun,' he continued, 'You'll have to have the stomach to use it. It ain't no use wavin' it in front of the man you're facin' hopin' to throw a scare into him. His aim is to kill you, unless you can down him first. Some men are born with the killin' instinct; some, it kinda grows on them; others never get it and they end up dead.' Joel grinned. 'You oughta do OK, marshal. You showed balls when you stood up to those two gunmen. Though I reckon the testin' time won't come for you. You'll probably have to do no more law enforcin' than cold-cockin' a rowdy drunk, or shoot down a mad dog.'

The icy look came into Joel's eyes again. 'Believe me, boy, you don't ever want to be cursed with the killin' lust. It can get a man an early grave as sure as the spotted plague can.'

He showed true grit all right at the shoot-out at the store, Jimmy thought bitterly. Who was he kidding? Mr Garretson or himself? He had almost been crapping himself hunkered down behind the packing cases with the gunmen's lead flying all around him. That he might one day be walking towards a bunch of professional *pistoleros*, by God, whose guns were notched with the tally of their kills gave him the shakes. Jimmy quickly changed the subject.

'How're you settling in at our place, Mr Garretson?' he asked. 'I have to tell you that my ma wasn't keen on having you as a lodger.'

Joel grinned. 'Well, your ma has just mended my shirt,' he replied. 'So I figure she's got over her dislike of me. I'm ridin' out to have words with the boss man of the Slash Y to see if he'll buy my piece of land off me.' He favoured Jimmy with a quizzical look. 'What sort of man is Mr McDowell? Did he get bits shot off him at Gettysburg makin' him a Yankee-hater like the old marshal here?'

'I don't rightly know, Mr Garretson,' Jimmy replied. 'I've heard he's a fair but firm man in his dealings. He ain't a stompin' man. His crew ride into town on pay days but he stays on the ranch. The only family he's got is a granddaughter, Miss Kathy. Her pa was Mr McDowell's only son who, along with his wife, Kathy's ma, died of smallpox, seven, eight years ago. Miss Kathy's growed up into a fine young woman and knows the cattle business as well as any ranch straw boss.

'Sometimes she comes into Little Springs with the ranch's supply wagon. I've heard that Mr McDowell wants her to go back East to some fancy girls' school but she wants to stay on at the ranch, do the chores her father would be doing if he had still been alive.'

Jimmy's face took on a vacant-eyed dreamy look and Joel guessed that Miss Kathy was some gal, least-ways in the young marshal's eyes.

Jimmy saw Mr Garretson smiling at him. He coloured up. 'There ain't anything goin' between me and Miss Kathy, Mr Garretson!' he blurted. 'Why old man McDowell would horsewhip me if I did anything but pass the time of day with his granddaughter.'

Joel's grin widened. 'But you're a fully fledged town marshal now, boy. The good people of this town have trusted you to uphold the law here-abouts. Your social standard has risen somewhat. M'be Rancher McDowell will look more kindly on you now, m'be enough to allow you to spark up to Miss Kathy.'

Jimmy was all set to mouth off another denying outburst when he realized that Mr Garretson was only ribbing him. He grinned instead. 'And I might end up being the fastest gun along both sides of the Brazos,' he said. 'I'd better concentrate on holding down the marshal's job, Mr Garretson. Occupying my mind with fanciful dreams ain't the best way to do that.'

'A wise decision, Marshal,' replied Joel, thinking of his own fanciful thoughts about Jimmy's mother. 'It pays to keep your mind honed on the job in hand, leave your fanciful dreams to when you're asleep.' He gave another smile. 'If I get the chance at the Slash Y I'll kinda let it drop that Little Springs has got a good-lookin', fast-shootin' kid as its new marshal. I reckon that news oughta stir up a young girl's curiosity. Enough, m'be, for her to saddle up her horse and come ridin' hell-for-leather into town to have a looksee at this fella.'

Jimmy grinned back at him. 'You do that, Mr Garretson, and our jailhouse is going to have its first Yankee prisoner. Then you can sit there thinking of all Ma's fine cookin' you're missing.'

'You've got me over a barrel, Marshal,' Joel said. 'My lips are buttoned up. So I'll see you at the eatin'-table tonight.' He turned and walked out of the office.

Jimmy followed him and stood on the porch and watched him ride out then he sat down in Marshal Tweedy's old armchair. He tilted it back against the office wall, drew his hat brim lower over his eyes, to hawk-eye the quietness of Main Street as though it was some wild end of trail cowtown. If only he had a chaw he would feel like a real seasoned lawman.

4

Joel cut off the well-beaten trail to the Slash Y to take another look at his legacy. His second sighting of it was even more depressing than his first view of the property. He could never reclaim his land back from nature; years of neglect by his late uncle had turned the farm into a wilderness. Though this time there was more signs of activity. A dozen or so cows were watering at the creek or chewing at the grass sprouting high in what had been the living-room of the shack.

A sudden movement from across the creek snapped off his morbid thoughts and the Winchester which had been lying handy across his saddle horn was whipped up into a firing position and sighted on the rider on the far ridge.

'Hey mister, I mean no harm!' the youthful rider called out in alarm, his hands raised high. 'I'm a ranch-hand nursin' those cows!'

'Sorry, boy,' replied Joel, lowering the rifle. 'I don't mean you no harm either. But old habits die hard. Where I hail from a man holds on to his rifle tighter than a mother holds on to her new-born child, with the quick wit to use it at any off-puttin' sound, if he wants to keep his hair on.' He grinned at the boy to put him at his ease. 'Your sudden showin' up on that rise kinda alarmed me. I take it you're a Slash Y rider?'

'That's right, mister,' the ranch-hand replied, lowering his hands, getting over the shock of gazing at the black death-dealing muzzle of a rifle brought into play by a bearded, horse-faced old goat faster than most men could draw out their pistol. He sensed fearfully he had been within a split second of being blown clear out of his saddle, as dead as they come. Just to be on the safe side he kept on his bank of the creek. The old man

51

was too twitching-nerved for his peace of mind.

'I'm on my way to talk to your boss, boy,' Joel said. 'This fine piece of growin' land those cows happen to be grazin' on now belongs to me, Mr Joel Garretson. It was left to me by my old uncle. And by the state of the place he didn't raise any sweat keepin' it into shape. I was hopin', bein' that your boss is already runnin' his cows on it, he'll buy the land off me.'

'I dunno about that, Mr Garretson,' the ranch-hand replied. 'I only look after Mr McDowell's cows; I ain't privy to his business affairs. I'm Jonty Spears by the way.' Then feeling confident now that the old man was friendly, he kneed his horse across the creek and rode up to him.

'There's no need for you to ride all the way to the ranch big house, Mr Garretson,' he said. 'Mr McDowell's branding on the south range no more than a mile from here. I'll take you to him.' He grinned. 'That's if you don't mind the boss's cows eating your grass and drinking your water.'

'I don't mind, Mr Spears; at least the place is of some use,' Joel said. 'I ain't no sodbuster, but lookin' at that so-called *farm* is breakin' my heart. I can't get it off my hands soon enough. You take me to your boss.'

★   ★   ★

As they rode closer to the fire, Joel saw that there were four men, lean-faced ranch-hands, doing the roping and branding of the calves. A man dressed in an old, dark-coloured store suit and wearing a straw, wide-brimmed plains hat was eyeing all that was going on. Joel reckoned he was Mr McDowell, the owner of the Slash Y. He wasn't a big made man but Joel also opined the old rancher must have been big in the tough stakes to boss a spread of hard men if the rest of his crew were like the branding team.

There was someone else at the fire,

loosening the rope off the calf's legs after it had been branded, the girl Marshal Slatts had strong thoughts about, Miss Kathy McDowell. Though she was dressed in well-worn Levis, a thick plaid shirt and spurred boots, they did little to hide her well-curved, youthful figure.

Jumping clear of a wild-kicking maverick, her drooping-brimmed hat fell off and long, sun-bleached hair fell in a yellow cascade on to her shoulders and Miss McDowell became all female. And Joel knew why the kid marshal had got himself worked up thinking about her.

'This fella wants to see you, Mr McDowell,' Jonty called out, as he and Joel drew up their mounts. 'A Mr Garretson; he's now the owner of the old homestead at Willow Creek.'

Jonty dismounted but Joel remained in his saddle until he was invited to step down. The rancher hadn't invited him to come and see him on his own land so until he knew he was welcome he would sit tight. He wanted to keep on the good side of the prospective buyer.

Ben McDowell turned and looked up at him. The old rancher's toughness was showing in his gaze, direct-eyed and unblinking. But Joel had been subjected to fish-eyed, hard-eyed and drop-dead looks from Sioux Crow, Blackfeet and white-eyes, especially Colonel George Armstrong Custer, and it hadn't put him out any. He touched the brim of his hat in greeting to the girl and gave what he hoped would be taken as a friendly smile by her pa.

'I ain't figurin' on takin' too much of your valuable time, Mr McDowell, so I'll come straight to the reason of me ridin' on your range,' Joel began. 'As the boy here says, I'm the new owner of the late Jeremiah Garretson's property.' Joel patted a pocket in his coat. 'I have the papers here to prove it. And not bein' a sodbuster, let alone a miracle worker, there ain't no way I'm goin' to get that apology of a farm into something I can live off so I'm givin' you, Mr McDowell, the first offer to buy the land off me. Though I ain't got any idea what it's worth. If I leave it to the lawyers to dispose of it for me, those forked-tongued sons . . . beggin' your pardon, miss, will fleece me as slick as any road agent would.'

Rancher McDowell was doing some weighing up of his own. The big stranger had the unnerving habit of not looking at him for more than a few seconds at a time. Though he seemed to be sitting easy in his saddle his gaze was searching all corners of the range, like a man who was expecting trouble coming his way. An owlhoot? He didn't think so. The tall man hadn't the shifty-eyed look of a border bad-ass. McDowell shrugged mentally. What the hell, he thought, the stranger's watchfulness was his own business. The land he wanted to sell was worth no more than the selling price of twenty or so cows. And, as the big man had said, if the Eastern lawyers got their greedy paws on the deeds to the land they would up the price.

'I think we can come to some arrangement about your property, Mr Garretson,' he said. 'We'll settle up the business up at the ranch house when we're finished here. That should be within the hour. You can ride on up there and wait for me, Mr Garretson, if that's OK.'

Joel grinned. 'Mr McDowell, Crowbait here has carried me all this way south from Montana. I reckon if I ask him nicely he'll haul me a few more miles. Just you point me in the right direction.'

'There's no need for me to do that, Mr Garretson,' the rancher replied. 'My granddaughter, Kathy, will take you there.'

Joel grinned inwardly. Young Marshal Slatts would willingly give his right arm to ride alongside Miss Kathy. Then he smiled for real. 'You lead the way, miss, Crowbait' s gettin' restless; he must be gettin' hungry.'

They had just lost sight of the branding fire when a curious Kathy said, 'Crowbait? That's an unusual name for a horse, Mr Garretson. And I've never seen a more leaner yet high-standing horse before.'

'That's bein' he's part Crow bred, Miss Kathy,' replied Joel. 'But Injuns favour smaller horses, ponies, they don't eat as much. Crowbait was a kinda throwback from a mare the Crow musta lifted off some Montana ranch and he grew too big for his Crow owner to feed. Come a real bad winter and old Crowbait would have ended up in the cookin' pot. I keep tellin' him how lucky he is gettin' a white-eye as an owner. Though give the critter his due he's got the stayin' power of an Injun pony, as long as I feed him well.'

Kathy saw Joel's face steel over at the same time as his horse snorted several times.

'Miss Kathy,' Joel said, in matter-of-fact voice. 'Do you get much Indian trouble?'

'Indian trouble?' Kathy repeated. 'Never this close to the home range, Mr Garretson.' Disturbed by the big man's hard-lined face she looked nervously about her then made to pull her mount round to make a mad dash back the way they had come.

'It's no use, missy,' Joel said. 'The red devils would run us down in a matter of minutes. They're in that dry wash away to our left.'

Kathy couldn't resist casting a fearful glance in the direction of the wash, hoping against hope, seeing no signs of any hostiles, that Mr Garretson was imagining it all. Though the unchanging hardness in his features told her otherwise.

Joel smiled reassuringly at the ashen-faced, lip-trembling girl. 'They ain't roped us in yet,' he said. 'I won't let them harm you, I promise.' He didn't tell the girl that preventing the Indians from harming her could mean that he would have to shoot her dead. Though being a plains-raised girl he guessed she would know the grim significance of his promise. 'We'll pull up here and let the Indians show themselves and make up plans then.'

With a face like death itself, Kathy nudged her horse closer to Mr Garretson's before tugging at the reins. She realized that she was facing certain death, slow and painful and humiliating if taken alive by the Comanche, or a speedier one by Mr Garretson's gun. Yet the big man spoke of coming up with a plan that would allow her to escape either of those terrible fates. Or was Mr Garretson just trying to comfort her?

For the second time, Kathy was beginning to think that Mr Garretson, and Crowbait, had been mistaken about hostiles being close by. Then there the red devils were. Seven, eight of them, their ponies raising the dust as they rode out of the wash. She cried out aloud her fears.

Whether they were Apache, Comanche or Utes, Joel didn't exactly know, not being familiar with the southern plains Indians' get-up. Not that it made any difference, the red sons-of-bitches would kill him and the girl just as painfully as any Sioux or Crow. The man he had to win over was the warrior wearing the long feathered headdress of a minor chief. With a muffled, 'Stay there, missy,' Joel rode the few yards to confront the chief eyeball to eyeball. And close enough to see the puzzled, what-the-hell look the warrior was giving him back.

Joel remembered old 'Bearcoat' Miles telling him that if you went bold-assed up to an enemy who outnumbered you you could wrong-foot him and maybe swing the outcome of the action in your favour. One thing was for sure he was definitely outnumbered. He would have to try and save their lives by the power of his words.

He loosened his coat and ripped open his shirt showing the chief the faded tattoo of a bull's head on the left side of his chest then began to speak in the Lakota tongue with all the fervour he could muster. He didn't know if the Indian would be familiar with the Sioux language so he interposed his life or death oration with English hoping that his listener would get the gist of what he was saying. But he was banking on the chief knowing the old signs that had been used by the red man for hundreds of years, by tribes as far east as the timber-covered ridges of the Alleghenies. Like Christendom, all the Indian tribes had the same basic religious beliefs and gods, with some variations by tribal medicine men and shamans. He was gambling two lives on that being so.

'Chief,' he began, pointing at his tattoo. 'I am of the Bear clan of the Hunkpappas tribe whose kin are the Teton Sioux, the slayers of 'Yellow Hair' the blue-coat pony general in a great battle in a mountainous country your forefathers once hunted across before you built your villages in this barren land.' Joel had no doubts that the death of Custer whose 7th Cavalry wiped out a whole Cheyenne village on the Washita would have reached the loneliest Indian teppee, faster than the news of Abe Lincoln's assassination swept across the Union.

Joel laid on the half truths and downright lies thick and heavy, mentioning every shaman and chief he knew and heard of. He didn't tell the chief that some of the contacts he had made with the important warriors of the various tribes had been no closer than eye-balling them through the back sights of his rifle. The sweat poured off him as he got into his stride. He felt like some tree-stump politician seeking re-selection to the senate from a backwoods settlement. Only it was two lives he was after winning not votes.

'Since the killing of Yellow Hair all my blood brothers had fled north. I came south to your land as I was not willing to act as scout for the blue coats huntin' down my red brothers.'

Joel bold-eyed the Comanche chief to see if there was some positive signs on the stone-hewed face of what he had been telling him. Or if the red devil understood what he had been hearing. On the good side he had at least got the chief and his war-band's attention. They had made no aggressive move against him or the girl.

He jerked his thumb at Kathy, who he knew must be going through every kind of hell there was worrying about what he was up to. And realizing grimly that he would have to be one hell of a slick mover if all his fancy talk fell through and he had to keep his promise to the girl and shoot her before the chief stuck his lance through him.

'That girl is my squaw,' he said. 'A maiden who has cost many ponies. If it's your wish that I will not have the pleasure of deflowering her, then I demand, as a brother of the Bear clan, white-eye or not, to fight for my life in single combat with you or any warrior of your war-band.' He gimlet-eyed the chief. 'You have not forsaken the old ways, Chief?'

Now it was time to take one last desperate gamble, hoping that the old Shawnee he had wintered with in his soddy in a high valley in the Big Horns and had told him about Indian tribal law and beliefs hadn't been the ramblings of a half-drunk old man. Joel leaned forward in his saddle and gripped the surprised chief's left hand in a double-handed grip, pressing his left thumb into the Indian's palm. Accordingly to his cabin sharer it was a grip used by the teachers of the old secret ways to identify themselves to possible fellow members. A sign he was told WAS recognized beyond the great black water to the east.

Joel didn't give a hoot if the old signs were recognized in China. All he wanted them to do was to convince the cruel-faced son-of-a-bitch whose arm he was clutching that he was one with the red man. He would soon find out, and painfully, if the half-crazy old Shawnee had been telling him legends mixed up with facts.

Puzzlement, disbelief, then finally slow understanding swept across the chief's face. He wasn't one of the tribal elders who were keepers of the secret rituals of the Comanche but he remembered the stories the old warriors told across winter camp-fires of the ways of the Comanche and the Apache in the days when they fought the iron shirt invaders who rode up from the south with their fire sticks. It had taken some believing, but this white-eye knew the old signs and the beliefs. He was as much an Indian as he was.

He slewed round on his horse and spoke to his war band. In between the grunts and barks of the Comanche tongue he pointed his lance at Joel. At the end of his speech the warriors raised their bows, lances or rifles in a salute to him. Joel wanted to give a whoop or two and throw his hat into the air: he had been accepted for who he said he was. But Indian palaver was a serious business so he only raised his rifle in grateful acknowledgement.

On facing him again the chief said in English, solemn-voiced, 'You take your wife, brother of the Comanche nation, and go to her soon so that she shall present you with a son.' Face softening slightly he added, 'Beat her with a stout stick in the Indian way if she disobeys you or spoils your food.'

Joel felt confident and relieved enough to give a genuine smile. 'I'll do as you say, Chief. The ways of the white-eyes are weak.' With a last touch of his hat to the Comanche he turned Crowbait round and headed back to Kathy.

An anxious Kathy couldn't see any signs on Mr Garretson's face that things had gone well for them. And she began to wonder why the Indians had made no move against them. As he came, Kathy was sure he gave her a wink though he was still what the ranch-hands would call, po-faced.

'We're OK, missy,' Joel said, as he drew up Crowbait alongside her. 'But don't show any joy. I've fooled the chief, who is now my red brother, into believing that you're my recently bought wife and Injun squaws are supposed to look subdued when company is around. Now we're goin' to keep on foolin' him by makin' camp here until it's safe to ride out so step down and start collecting brushwood for a fire.' Joel gave her a tight-faced grin. 'That blood brother of mine says I've got to beat you with a stick if you ain't a good squaw. So if I holler at you it's only part of the show.'

A bewildered Kathy who had just gone through every emotion there was between abject terror and wild happiness swung down from her horse. She cast an apprehensive under-the-lids glance at the Indians sitting on their horses as unmoving as though carved from wood before she bent low and began gathering up kindling. Joel, as befitting a close brother of the red men, sat down and lit up a cigarette.

The chief gave a satisfied grunt, the Indian white-eye was treating his young squaw as a full-blood Indian would. He raised his right hand and gave several barking whoops of command and as one the war band swung their ponies round and vanished back down into the wash.

Joel gave his own grunt of satisfaction. He waited a few minutes before getting on to his feet and calling out, 'They've gone, missy! And it's time we were.'

Kathy didn't need telling twice. She dropped the brushwood and ran for her horse, leaping into the saddle as easily as any rodeo rider.

'You get goin',' Joel said as he mounted up. 'Crowbait ain't a sprinter so I'll follow your dust trail, I won't be far behind you. I've had enough of a scare to last me for a few years!'

Kathy smiled, something she thought she would never do again. 'Me too, Mr Garretson. I won't stop until I reach the ranch house.' She dug her heels into her horse's ribs with unusual savagery that set it off in a high-kicking, dust-raising gallop.

★   ★   ★

Rancher McDowell's worried expression lifted as he and the branding team thundered up to the big house and saw his daughter and Mr Garretson standing on the porch.

'You pair sure had me worried,' he said, as he dismounted. 'Me and the boys picked up the sign of a bunch of Comanche. We rode here as fast as we could. Did you see the tracks, Mr Garretson?'

'Oh we saw them, Pa,' Kathy said, before Joel could say his piece. Kathy's smile was forced this time as she reflected that she would never be so near to a fearful death again and be able to ride away from it. 'And it's thanks to Mr Garretson that they didn't butcher us.'

'Good Lord!' the rancher gasped then favoured Joel with a wondering-eyed look. 'How the heck did you do that?

Joel gave a self-effacing grin. 'I kinda

persuaded the chief that I was a white Injun.'

'A white Indian?' Ben McDowell's questioning-eyed look spread all over his face. 'I'm forgetting my manners, Mr Garretson. Let's go inside and you can tell me how you and a bloodthirsty Comanche kinda hit it off over a cup of coffee.'

'Well it's sort of a long story, Mr McDowell,' Joel began. He was sitting in the rancher's den enjoying fresh brewed coffee Kathy had made. The rancher kept glancing at his grand-daughter, thinking just how close he had been to losing her and what sort of magic the tall Yankee possessed to sweet-talk a Comanche chief into letting them go on their way unharmed.

'It was when I was a trapper in the high country of Montana before I was scout for the army,' Joel said. 'The snows came early that year, closing the passes so I couldn't make it back to Fort Burford and had to stick the winter out in the cabin. This day, the blizzards had eased off, I was out to see if there was anything worth shooting to help out the cabin's stores when I came across this old Indian lying in a crack in the face of a butte. I thought he had died of exposure, but when I found out he was still breathing, I carried him back to the cabin. He pulled through and stayed with me till the snows melted.'

Joel looked the rancher straight in the eyes. 'I don't know what your feelin's are against Injuns here in Texas, but I neither hate them or love them any more than I would any white man. But I'll tell you this, Mr McDowell, you have to thank an old Shawnee that your granddaughter is not bein' paraded about in some Comanche camp. And the old Injun gets my thanks for savin' my hair.'

'Shawnee?' exclaimed a surprised McDowell. 'Where the hell's their stompin' ground, Mr Garretson?'

'That had me puzzled at first,' Joel replied. 'I've had dealin's with the

Crow, Sioux, Blackfeet and Cheyenne, life or death dealin's I might add, but I'd never clapped eyes on a Shawnee. And I have to tell you this, Mr McDowell, he was the craziest Injun I'd ever met. He spoke good English and he told me how the Great Spirit of the Injun people must have sent me to save his life so he could continue with his mission.'

'What mission was that, Mr Garretson?' the rancher asked, his curiosity aroused.

'Well,' Joel said, 'The old man told me the Shawnee lodges were in the Alleghenies a long, long ways from where I found him and that he was the boss medicine man of the Shawnee nation, and that the same Great Spirit who had sent me to save him, had told him in a dream that he oughta leave the land of the Shawnee and spread the true Injun gospel, so to speak, to the back-slidin' tribes of the Great Plains. How the heck he knew there were Indians that far west I don't know. But he was crazy enough to go on the journey, and crazy enough to other Injuns on his trek for them not to kill him.'

'He's no more loco than some of our own preachers, Mr Garretson,' the rancher said. 'Trying to convert the white-eye-hating Indians to our faith.'

'Was it the old Shawnee who taught you all the signs you made to that Comanche chief, Mr Garretson?' Kathy said.

'He sure did, missy,' replied Joel, grinning. 'All through that winter old Kaysinata, that's the closest I can get to his name, gave me the lowdown on medicine men, shamans, who were preachin' the words of the Great Spirit when the redcoats was fightin' the French. He told me of their secret rites and signs until I reckon I could go to one of those fine Eastern schools and write a book about them. He also mentioned in passing that it was a great honour for a white man to hear such things, but that I was no ordinary white man, I had been a messenger from the

Great Spirit. See this!' Joel opened his shirt and bared his chest and showed the the rough drawn tattoo of a bull. He grinned. 'Occasionally I used to partake of the demon drink, to kinda while away the long winter nights. Kaysinata wouldn't even look at the bottle. One morning when I woke up after a heavy session, my chest hurt like hell and I found out that the old Injun had carved this on my chest. I ain't a religious man, Mr McDowell, I don't pander to the Injun way of thinkin' that a man's life pattern is already written down someplace. I believe what misfortune happens to a fella is because he's in the wrong place at the wrong time. Yet that old man who had walked all the way from the Ohio told me that that mark would protect me. It certainly did that.'

'Amen to that,' whispered Kathy, as she realized it must have been a miracle: an Indian one, that had saved her and Mr Garretson from a fearful dying.

'What Kaysinata told me,' continued

Joel, 'was that the tattooed bull was the sign of Sitting Bull's clan. Sitting Bull, as you may know, Mr McDowell, is the boss medicine man of the whole Sioux Nation. Now how the heck did that old devil know that when he told me he had never met any Sioux in his wanderin's in Montana? It sure has me puzzled. I reckon I should start believin' in the Injuns' 'Book of Life', Mr McDowell.'

'Where is Kaysinata now, Mr Garretson?' asked Kathy.

'He left the cabin as soon as the passes were open,' replied Joel. 'So if he's still alive he must be preachin' the true religion to the Sioux and the Crow.' He grinned. 'That's enough of my life story, Mr McDowell, let's get down to the business at hand, the sellin' of my land at a price that suits us both.'

'Before we get down to business, Mr Garretson,' replied the rancher. 'I want to thank you for saving my granddaughter's life. She's all the family I've got left. I will always be beholden to you.'

Joel raised a hand in protest. 'Hold it

there, Mr McDowell,' he said. 'I kinda saved my own life in the process so there ain't no need for you to be owin' me.'

Rancher McDowell eyed Joel for several seconds without speaking. Finally he said, 'You have ridden a long way, Mr Garretson, for a hope that's gone sour on you. If you are keen to stay here in the Brazos I'll see to it that your trip will have been worthwhile. My boys will rebuild the cabin; there's plenty of good timber hereabouts, and they're used to building line cabins. Then we'll get your land ready for planting.'

'I ain't seekin' any favours for savin' my own neck, Mr McDowell,' Joel said.

'It's not a favour, Mr Garretson,' replied the rancher. 'It's what I figure I owe you for all the grazing time my cows have spent eating your grass.'

'You stay, Mr Garretson, please,' Kathy said. 'We can put you up here at the ranch, can't we, Grandpa, till your place is built? Regardless of what you said about saving your own life you did save mine and I wouldn't be happy to see you ride off to God knows where without the McDowells showing you our thanks.'

It was Joel's time to sit for a few moments without speaking as he did some rapid thinking. He smiled at Kathy. 'Miss McDowell,' he said. 'Putting it like that I reckon I oughta stay. I might tell you I was hankerin' to put my roots down here, like staying in one place, livin' under a roof. But I'll have to turn down your kind offer of beddin' down here at the ranch. I've already got a room with Mrs Slatts, she's a widow woman, the young town marshal's mother.'

'I don't mean to be personal, Mr Garretson,' the rancher said, 'but if you run out of cash you can always tend cows for me.'

Joel laughed. 'Crowbait's too old to take up bein' a cow pony, Mr McDowell, and I ain't got the backbone to last out a day as a ranch-hand.' He grinned. 'If I am pushed for cash I'll tend bar or get a job as the marshal's deputy. Though I'm reckonin' on ridin' out to the crick and give your boys a hand buildin' my cabin.' He stood up. 'It's time I got back to Little Springs, thanks for the coffee, and the help, Mr McDowell, it's much appreciated.' He looked down at Kathy, favouring her with a narrow-eyed gaze. 'You stay close to the ranch for the future; no more ridin' out on your ownsome. It might have been just accidental that bunch of Comanche comin' this close to the ranch. Or the red devils could be comin' more bold, lookin' for something to lift from the white-eyes.'

Kathy gave a involuntary shudder followed by a whispered, 'I will, Mr Garretson, I will.'

Mr McDowell got to his feet and shook Joel's hand. 'It'll be a coupla days before I can get a team organized,' he said. 'But being it's your property they're building you're welcome to say your piece how you want the shack built. I'll let my straw boss, Seth, know to act on any suggestions you might make, Mr Garretson.'

★   ★   ★

Joel was taking the Comanche threat seriously. On the ride back to Little Springs he was all ears and eyes for Indian sign. He grinned as he noticed that Crowbait's ears were prodding the air. He was taking the threat just as seriously.

5

Marshal Tweedy groaned with pain as he eased himself up on his pillow. The bandages were strapped that tight across his chest he could hardly breathe.

'You were lucky, Bill,' Doc Baxter had told him. 'You took three slugs and you lost a heap of blood but they passed clean through you. If that Yankee hadn't put paid to those two gunmen and helped young Slatts to get you to my surgery you would have been as dead as poor old Benson. That boy showed true grit. He took on those killers before the Yankee showed up.'

Then the old goat told him he had to just lie there and recuperate. Grinning he added, 'Marshal Slatts ought to be able to keep the peace in town until you're up and about again.'

His young deputy upholding the law?

The marshal gave a sour-faced look. Then cursed himself for his uncharitable thought towards someone who had helped to save his life. And he would have to thank the big Yankee for backing up the boy at risk to his own life. Fate, Marshal Tweedy thought, was a peculiar thing. A Yankee had shot a lump out of his leg, another Yankee had saved his life. And he would also have to apologize to him for his churlishness towards him at their first meeting. He hadn't exactly given the Yankee a southern hospitable welcome. 'Doc!' he called out. 'Can you do me a favour?'

Jimmy Slatts gave Joel the message that Marshal Tweedy wanted to see him when he rode into town from the creek, feeling much happier now that he had seen the Slash Y crew starting on the rebuilding of his new home.

Joel grinned. 'Well I'd better go and pay him a visit, Marshal. I don't want to upset him any more than I seem to have done already in case he orders you to run me outa town.'

As he walked along the street to the surgery, Joel began to wonder how far a man had to ride to get out of reach of shooting trouble, to be able to live the rest of his life at ease with his neighbours. Little Springs had seemed such a place he was seeking yet within a couple of days he'd had to gun down two hard-cases and sweat his balls off pleading with a bunch of white-eye haters to save his and a young girl's life. Was it written in that Book of Life old Kaysinata spoke of that trouble would always ride alongside him? Then Joel thought of the sweet-smiling Widow Slatts and decided that things hadn't been all troublesome in his new territory.

Joel got another pleasant feeling when he walked into Marshal Tweedy's sickroom. After thanking him for saving his life, the old marshal apologized for his earlier ill-mannered greeting of him. 'It's just that I'm a cantankerous old cuss,' he said, 'who ain't got the savvy to accept that the damn blasted war is over.'

Joel smiled down at the lawman. 'Hard words don't break bones, Marshal,' he said. 'And it wasn't only me who saved your life. Your young deputy stood his ground and faced the sonsuvbitches.'

'Yeah, I know that,' replied the marshal. 'The boy showed balls out there on the street and I ain't about to sell him short, Mr Garretson, but he ain't a full fledged peace officer yet. Owlhoots like the two assholes you shot could pass this way again.' The marshal thin-smiled. 'I know I ain't got the right to ask you to do this what with me being an ex-reb, but I'd be obliged if you'd kinda watch over Marshal Slatts, when you're in town that is. Until I get back on to my feet.'

'I'll look out for the boy, Marshal, never fear,' replied Joel. 'I've already promised his ma I would do just that. It'll pass the time away while I'm waitin' for the Slash Y crew to rebuild my shack.'

Marshal Tweedy gasped. 'How the

hell did you get old Ben McDowell to pull his men off tendin' his cows to do that?'

'Mr McDowell felt that he was kinda beholden to me,' Joel said, straight-faced. 'So you can take it that you'll have a goddamned Yankee livin' close by you.' He turned and left the room, leaving Marshal Tweedy puzzling why Ben McDowell owed the Yankee a favour when he couldn't have known him for more than an hour or so. And why the Widow Slatts had been so forthcoming enough to ask a stranger to keep an eye on her boy? As well as men dying fast in Mr Garretson's presence, events moved fast as well.

6

Ed Megan sat at a small fire in the middle of a thick patch of brush and mesquite. His gang had just pulled off another succesful raid and the thirty or so horses they had netted were being driven by two of his men to rendezvous with Carlos, a *comanchero jefe* in a cash-on-delivery exchange. All in all, Megan thought, it had been a wise decision on his part to quit Missouri and come south-west to the border territory of New Mexico.

Megan was a burly, bearded, shut-faced man and, as befitting a former wartime Missouri guerilla, was well armed for any sudden eventuality. Belted across his ample belly were two holstered long-barrelled .44 Walker Colt pistols, a smaller calibre pistol was in a pocket of his stained duster. Slung across his left shoulder and chest was a bandoleer of brass-cased reloads for the fifteen-shot Winchester lying by his side.

Back there in Missouri, though the war had been lost over ten years before, guerilla hold-outs like the James and the Younger boys still kept up the fight against the hated Union by robbing banks and heisting trains. The armed men hunting them down, Union troops, regular lawmen and Pinkertons, in the tangled backwoods, were roping in, or shooting on sight, any man who could be identified, rightly or wrongly, as a former guerilla fighter, even if he was walking behind his plough.

Megan had had to spend most of his post-war life holed up in damp caves like some hunted animal until the posses had moved out of the territory and he could get back to his dirt farm. His hatred of the Southern politicians, men whom he had killed for, men who had betrayed the guerillas by putting a price on their heads after the war, burned inside him like a belly ulcer.

Megan was discussing the quality, or lack of it, of their lives since the end of the war with Milt Hogg and Bob Fowler, men who had ridden alongside him with Quantrill during the war. At the latest warning that several Pinkertons were nosing around the woods close by their holdings, they were hiding in a cave with the smell of its owner still strong in their nostrils.

'We could've started robbin' banks, Ed,' Milt said. 'If the James and the Youngers hadn't set up such a fuss in Missouri with their bank robberies. Why, a man could get himself plugged stealin' a candy bar from some crossroad store.'

Megan stopped his stone-faced gazing at the wet wind-lashed trees and turned and looked at Bob and Milt with some purpose showing on his face. He saw them sitting there with rain dripping off their slickers, sodden, drooping, brimmed hats, haunted eyes set deep in gaunt-boned faces. He had seen more lively-looking corpses.

'You might have something there,' Milt said. 'We may have been sodbusters before the war but we learned the raidin' and killin' trade ridin' with Quantrill. I reckon if the James and the Younger boys can heist banks, we can. But we'll start up our raidin' long ways from Missouri and the goddamned Pinkertons. Though the way I see it, it ain't robbin' it's part payment from the South for what we did in the war and the hell they've put us through since old Bob Lee told us to quit fightin'. Are you with me, boys?'

'I'm with you, Ed,' said Bob speaking for the first time. 'I'll ride with you any place on this God's earth as long as we get out this cave before whatever we chased out comes back with some of its buddies.'

It didn't take long to pack up what gear they had and say their goodbyes to their families. It had been a commonplace chore saying their farewells since before the war when free-soilers and pro-slavers where conducting their own war along the Kansas/Missouri border country, every bit as bloody as the big war to come. Taking advantage of the rain and the darkness to shield them from any watchful-eyed Pinkertons, they rode south along faint traces only known by men born and bred in the backwoods, into Indian Territory.

Before crossing over the line into the Texas Panhandle, Megan recruited eight ex-rebs who had served under General Jeb Stuart, men who had lost everything during the war but their stubborn pride and their guns, and the willingness, Ed discovered, to use them to get their wherewithal. Megan now had a gang to raise hell with in New Mexico.

Using the well-tried tactics of the Missouri brush boys, going in fast and unexpected, taking what they wanted by the gun, the knife or flaming torch, then hightailing it out again, they made their first raid.

The ranch house had been in complete darkness though there was a lighted lantern hanging above the bunkhouse door when they struck. Two flame-sparking torches arcing across the night sky, one smashing through a window in the big house, the other landing on the flat tinder-dry tarp-covered roof of the crew's quarters, were the heralds of a small massacre about to take place.

Within minutes flames were licking out of the windows of the house and, fanned by the strong wind, they were spreading rapidly across the roof of the bunkhouse. Without any given word of command, three of the raiders cut off to the horse corral at the rear of the house, the ranch's remuda, the reason for the raid. The rest of the gang covered the house and the bunkhouse. Shirtless, bootless, pantless, half asleep ranch-hands jostled each other as they staggered out of the bunk house. Before they could work out how the fires had started they were cut down in a hail of lead. It was a likewise fate for the three people, one of them a female, who burst, coughing and spluttering on to the porch of the house.

Helped along by whooping reb cries and pistol shots the horses, nostrils dilated with fear, raised the dust high as they thundered out of the corral. Megan watched them hightailing it along the trail. He gave a satisfied grunt. Quantrill, he opined, couldn't have carried out the raid any slicker.

'OK, boys!' he yelled. 'We're finished here, let's get to hell out of it!'

Now the gang had three years of raiding behind them. One time they would heist some small-town's bank in New Mexico, a few weeks later, a ranch in Arizona would be raided. They were confusing the law in where they would strike next as much as General 'Stonewall' Jackson did to the Union forces seeking him during the war. Yet their success was slowing them down.

Other than the contents of bank safes and payroll-carrying stages the gang only stole horses, animals that could be driven faster than longhorns and were more valuable. But it took time to find a trader who wouldn't look too closely at brand marks of the stock he was being offered, or demand such legal niceties as bills of sale — always providing that they could move the stolen horses along the trail without meeting up with a marshal's posse.

Megan had thought about this problem for quite a while before he came up with a likely solution. The *comancheros*, a band of Mexicans, 'breeds, full-blood Indians and white renegades operating out of the wild badlands of the Llana Estacado of New Mexico, were men like himself who lived by thieving, though they stole anything which could be of value to them, gold, silver, horses, cattle, guns, women and children, killing those they had no use for. Their leader was a Mexican called Carlos.

Maybe, Megan had opined, Carlos would buy the horses the gang lifted. He would probably have to lower the price he wanted for them, but it would be a quicker sale and a lot less dangerous than looking round for buyers themselves. First, though, he had to make contact with the *comanchero* chief.

Megan left word at the village cantinas frequented by the owlhoot fraternity that a Mr Megan would like a meeting with Carlos at a place of his choosing. Stressing that Mr Megan was in the same business as Carlos was, he wanted to discuss a trading proposal with him which would be financially beneficial to both of them.

Carlos got the message. He had heard of a gang of gringo *bandidos* who had suddenly appeared in New Mexico and who had made a name for themselves by robbing banks and stages as far west as Arizona, and for gringo *bandidos*, were not averse to killing to get what they wanted. Carlos cold-smiled, as his *muchachos* did. Carlos decided he would meet this gringo, Señor Megan, whom he took to be the *jefe* of the gringo *bandidos*. Any enterprise that brought him gain was interesting.

A cry of, 'Rider comin' in!' brought Megan to his feet, picking up his Winchester as he did so. The gang was holed-up in a knife slash of a canyon that cut deep into the mountain. There was water and grass for the horses here and, more importantly, a goat track of a trail of an escape route clinging to the face of the rock wall at the end of the canyon. Megan levered a shell into the chamber of the Winchester. This place was as safe a camp as anywhere in the territory, but it didn't do for men with dead-or-alive prices on their heads to relax their guard. One man could be the point rider for a whole bunch of badge-wearing riders.

Another shout of, 'It's OK, boys, it's only Bob!' eased the tension out of Megan. Bob had been making the rounds of the cantinas to see if Carlos had replied favourably to his suggestion of a meeting. A grinning Bob gave him the answer he had been hoping for before he had dismounted and spoke to him.

'Carlos has sent word he'll meet us at Black Rock canyon,' Bob said. 'The Mex cantina owner says it's about two hours' ride north of here.'

'Good,' replied Ed. 'Now we've got to ask ourselves can we trust the Mex, Bob? He'll have figured out who I am and that there's a price on our heads; the bastard could turn us in. I also reckon Carlos will show up at the canyon with a bunch of his men and by what we've heard of the wild ways of the *comancheros* they'll be a bunch to be reckoned with.' Megan gave Bob a hard-eyed look. 'Will Carlos play straight with us, Bob?'

Bob Fowler hated all Yanks, Mexicans, Negroes, Indians and mixed-blood men. Ed opined he was the most hating man he had ever known and asking him to trust a Mexican was like asking him to walk into the nearest marshal's office and give himself up to pay for all his robbing and killing.

'You know I ain't partial to even passin' the time of day with a stinkin' greaser, Ed, let alone trust one, but bein' I can see that a deal with this fella Carlos can be in our favour, I'll put aside my dislikes. Though I ain't about to trust him not to try and pull a fast one on us if the sonuvabitch thinks he can get away with it. So I figure, just to make sure we ain't caught napping, me and Matt and a couple of the boys haul ourselves to this canyon and get bedded down along the rimline.' Bob gave a death's-head grimace of a smile. 'If that greaser *jefe* so much as farts outa turn why we'll just cut loose at him and the no-good scum he's brung with him with our Winchesters.'

Ed's grin was just as cheerless. 'I was just considerin' the same kinda plan, Bob. We can't let some penny-ante greaser bastard outsmart a bunch of hard-ridin' brush boys. You move out as soon as you're ready, Carlos could be reckonin' on puttin' some of his own boys on the ridges.'

★ ★ ★

Carlos and twenty of his *muchachos*, still mounted on their horses, were in a rough semi-circle 200 yards in Diablo Canyon when the seven gringo *bandidos* came into view. They were riding in a double column like a Federale patrol with the *hombre* who must be their *jefe* at the head of them.

Carlos gave a smirk of satisfaction. Counting the riflemen he had hidden in the rocks at either side of the trail his band outnumbered the gringo dogs by almost four to one. The price he would get bringing them in dead would be easier earned, and more profitable, than stealing horses and cattle.

Then suddenly Carlos's sharp-honed self-preservation nerves began to twitch. He was beginning to get a gut-chewing feeling that he had underestimated the gringo *bandido jefe*. He hadn't played into his hands. He wasn't seeing all the *hombres* in the Yankee gang. He glanced nervously up at at both sides of the canyon.

'Yes, you greaser bastard,' Ed muttered to himself, as he kneed his horse close up to Carlos. 'You were all set to double-cross us, but now it don't seem such a good idea to you right now, unless you're keen to shed a lot of Mex blood.' He favoured the *comanchero jefe* with a wide, but forked-tongued smile.

'It's a real pleasure to meet you, Mr Carlos,' he said. 'I'm hopin' me and you can do business together. The deal I have in mind will make money for both of us with my boys takin' all the risks. Though I'll admit some of the boys ain't overjoyed doin' business with a greas — a Mexican. I told them that Mr Carlos is a businessman and if he sees that he can make money without raisin' any sweat, by hell, he'll not turn the deal down without hearin' me out. But I didn't convince them, Mr Carlos, they're up there on the high ground coverin' you and your boys with their

Winchesters just to make sure our discussions are carried out peaceful like.' Ed fixed a beady-eyed stare on Carlos. 'That none of us go off at half-cock and do something we'll regret startin'.'

Carlos's gaze flashed upwards again and Ed saw the glint of fear in the black shoe-button eyes set deep in a heavily jowled face. Carlos's unease spread to his men and Ed heard the squeak of leather as they twisted ass in their saddle, and, like their *jefe*, looked up at the rims of the canyon.

Ed was doing some fear-sweating himself. He was worried that just for the sheer hell of it Bob would cut loose with his rifle at Carlos then there would be one quick, but bloody, shoot-out taking place in the canyon.

Carlos took a final look upwards. This hard-faced gringo dog was willing to take on his *muchachos* in a gunfight although, he guessed, even counting the unseen riflemen on the canyon rim, his men outnumbered the Yankees. But he knew that the gringos were loco. Not wishing to be as crazy as them and risk this place becoming his early grave, he forgot about his idea of collecting the bounty on the gringo *bandidos*.

Yet his meeting with Señor Megan need not have been a long wasted ride. The gringo *jefe* had mentioned easily earned money with no risks to him or any of his men in the taking of it. Swallowing his disappointment and loss of face at things not working out the way he had wanted, he said, 'Tell me of this plan of yours, Señor Megan, which will bring me much *dinero* for so little effort.' Carlos's smile was as wide and just as false as Ed's had been.

* * *

They had been trading stolen horses for gold and silver for over two years, Carlos even allowing them to hide out in his stronghold in the high wilderness of the Llana Estacado when the law were pressing the gang too hard. There they could relax, get drunk and enjoy the pleasures of soft-fleshed, hot-blooded *señoritas*. Yet in spite of all Carlos's outward showing of friendliness, Ed, like Bob, didn't trust the *comanchero* leader. He knew, if it suited Carlos's purpose, he would sell out his 'gringo amigos'.

Megan threw the dregs of his coffee on the fire and got to his feet. He looked down at Bob and Milt stretched out on the other side of the fire.

'Boys,' he said. 'I'm gettin' the feelin' we've done enough robbin' in this part of the territory. Twice this week we've seen the trail dust of marshals' posses. There's no need to push our luck, there's plenty banks to rob and horses to steal the other side of the Pecos across in Texas. And if we quit liftin' horses, we won't have to find a way to get them back to our good buddy, Carlos, and that will allow us to move around faster.'

'I was goin' to suggest a move elsewhere myself, Ed,' Bob said. 'It ain't only the law that's got me worried but that sonuvabitch Carlos. The last time we rode into his camp I could see by the look on his ugly face he was workin' out how much gold we're worth if he hauled us in dead to a town marshal's office. There'll come a time, Ed, as sure as I'm lyin' here when we ain't his amigos, any more. And that just ain't my natural hatred towards greasers spoutin' forth.'

'How about you, Milt?' Ed asked, po-faced. 'Are you ready for a change of *señoritas*?'

Milt grinned. 'I figure there oughta be plenty females in Texas willin' and able to cool down a randy dog of a Missourian.'

'I reckon there will, Milt,' replied Ed. 'Now stop lyin' there thinkin' about them and get mounted up, and catch up with Pat and Lester. Tell them to let the men Carlos has sent to collect the horses know we're quittin' doin' business with him for a spell. But we'll start tradin' with him again when we come back from Texas.'

Carlos sat in his cabin doing some hard thinking, ignoring the wine and food his current bed companion had placed on the table, after he had heard that his gringo partners were ending their business deal with him. It had been a deal that had been a favourable one to him and one he did not want ending, leastways not on his gringo partners' say-so. The ending of the deal he had in mind was when he killed all of the gringo gang like any law-abiding citizen would do then claim the reward on their bodies.

For several minutes he sat, scowling-faced, trying to come up with a plan that would still have the gringos, even as far away as Texas, of financial benefit to him. Carlos's scowl slowly changed into a shadow of a smile then into a broad fierce grin. The gringo dogs didn't know it but they were still partners, only they wouldn't be getting their cut of the deal he had in mind. He got to his feet and walked across to the open doorway and yelled, '*Chaco, venaqui, pronto!*'

A lean-figured man with the cold-eyes and the sharp features of a part-blood Indian, jumped up from a nearby camp and hurried across to his *jefe*.

'The gringo *bandidos* are riding into Texas, Chaco,' Carlos said. 'Pick up their trail where they ford the Pecos and follow it until they've crossed the border, so you can tell me if they intend raiding north or south of the Texas line, *comprende?*'

The 'breed nodded. '*Si, mi patron,*' he said, and turning, ran to his horse and leapt on its back to ride out of the stronghold bare-backed as his Yaqui father would have done on his *jefe's* mission.

Carlos stepped back into the shack and sat down at the table again and poured himself a glass of wine and began to eat with the satisfaction of a man well pleased with himself. He had always wanted to lead his *muchachos* in a raid against the hated Texans. Along with the cattle and horses a sudden raid would get him, there would be many gringo women and children for the taking, trade goods an Indian *jefe* would willingly buy. Why he hadn't raided into Texas before was the fact that Carlos had a high respect for the deadly man-hunting capabilities of the dreaded Texas Rangers.

Now there was a safe way into Texas for his war band. While the gringo lawmen were busy trying to track down Señor Megan and his gang he would make one quick in-and-out raid well clear from that activity. Carlos's smile was softer now as he thought of the delights a gringo virgin would bring him during the cold winter nights, with the added pleasure that it was the gringo dogs who had made him lose face at Diablo Canyon who were making his raid possible.

7

Ed, Bob and Lester rode along the hardpan track of a Main Street sitting easy in their saddles as though they had nothing more on their minds than downing several glasses of beer in the saloon, towards the double-storeyed, adobe building with iron bars fixed on all its ground-floor windows, the Stockman's Association bank.

Milt and Bud and two more of the gang had been in Carlsberg for over an hour. Milt and Bud were in the Drovers' Saloon, the only bar in the town, playing cards at a table near a street window that gave them a clear pistol-shot view on the marshal's office across the street, where trouble would come boiling out of if any shooting had to be done to get hold of the bank's cash, trouble that would end in the marshal and his deputy's deaths before their running feet hit the street.

The other two raiders stood at the bar drinking but ready to swing round to discourage any of the other six drinkers in the saloon who felt concerned enough to try and prevent their bank from being robbed by dashing out and joining up with the marshal. Discouraging a suchlike foolhardy man the way the Megan gang operated, meant gunning him down.

The remaining four members of the gang were lying in ambush at the end of the small wooden bridge that spanned a narrow but sheer-sided wash. They were the holding back men. Four rapid-firing long guns would raise havoc among any hot-pursuing posse-men who would have to bunch up to get over the narrow bridge. Then those of the posse who weren't shot dead and still had the balls to hunt down the gang, would have to ride a mile east until the bank lowered enough for a horse to negotiate the crossing of the wash without breaking a leg or its rider's neck.

By then the giveaway trail dust of the main body of raiders would have dispersed and they would be well hidden in one of the numerous canyons that cut into the mountain where a nose-to-the-ground Indian tracker would fail to pick up their trail.

As they drew up their mounts in front of the bank, Ed went quickly through his tactics needed to pull off a successful bank heist, and he couldn't find fault with them. Though being a seasoned raider he knew that if any shooting started, even the best thought out plans tend to go all to hell. But that situation would have to be played out as it came.

Riding south-east once they had cleared the Texas border, they spotted the cluster of buildings of a small town and the gang immediately went to ground, Ed reasoning that the crews of the close-by spreads would be known in the town. If that wasn't the case, his boys were too well armed to pass as ranch-hands. He didn't want to arouse the town marshal's suspicions that a band of outlaws was riding into his town until the bank manager was standing on the bank's porch yelling out that his bank had been robbed.

Ed waited for Bob, who had been sent into the town to see if it had a bank or a store, or whatever, worthwhile for the gang to ride in and rob it, then make their presence known in this neck of Texas to the Rangers and the ensuring hell that would raise.

Bob had come back with good news. 'We've struck gold here, Ed,' he said, as he dismounted, grinning widely. 'There's a bank in that dog-dirt town and only an old fart of a marshal and one deputy to stop us from robbin' it. And that ain't all the good news, Ed: I reckon you saw that east-bound stage roll into town?'

'Yeah, we saw it,' replied Ed. 'It must have been the regular Butterfield stage heading for California; what good news is that?'

'That stage pulled up outside the bank before carryin' on to the stage depot and the shotgun guard dismounted and lugged a strongbox inside the bank.' Bob's smile stretched to his ears. 'Now there can only be one thing carried in a strongbox, Ed, money! Gold, or the paper variety.'

Ed's smile wasn't as broad as Bob's but it held some warmth. 'It could be holdin' the pay for the ranch-hands on those cattle spreads we rode over since we crossed the border. It looks like we're in business, Bob. Grab yourself a mug of coffee then tell me the layout of the bank so we can plan the safest and fastest way to get our hands on that cash.'

And now here they were, Ed thought, about to pull off their first heist in Texas, and one that had the look of paying off well. Yet within a few minutes of Bob and him walking into the bank he quickly realized how wrong his thoughts had been.

It was a small bank with only two teller positions: one served by an elderly man, the other by a young girl. Seeing no other bank employee behind the counter grill, Ed took the man to be the bank manager. Beyond the counter, Ed saw that the bank's safe door was open. The only customer in the bank was a stooped-backed old man with plainsman-length white hair wearing a black frock-coat and an Abe Lincoln stovepipe hat. Ed grinned at Bob. It would be like getting money from home. Both of them stopped just inside the bank and drew out their pistols.

'Howdy folks,' Ed said. 'Me and my pard have come to rob this bank, but there ain't no call for any of you to get hurt in the process.' Ed's voice lost its conversational tone. 'But we're pre-pared to kill if we have to, even you, missy.' Ed fixed a hard-eyed stare at the white-faced girl teller. 'Now, hand over the cash from that strongbox the stage dropped off here without any fuss then the bank can get back to doin' its normal business.'

'And you, old-timer,' a grinning Bob said, talking to the round-shouldered customer, 'you ain't about to give us any trouble, are you?'

'I'll give you trouble, you no-good white trash,' Colonel Bradley Shelby muttered under his breath. During the war he had led a company of Texas riflemen in an attack on the Devil's Den, a Union strong-point in their battle line at Gettysburg. He had come staggering back to the Confederate lines wounded in four places and minus half his command. He had faced a double line of rifle fire that day and had not been found wanting. Two pistols aimed at him were of no concern.

He turned slowly and faced the smiling bank robber holding a pistol loosely on him. Bob's smile faded fast and for two fatal seconds he froze as he saw the long-barrelled pistol the old man held in his right hand. He was too close to hear the discharge of the shell that blew most of the back of his head away but he did see its blinding flash before the everlasting blackness of death engulfed him.

Before Bob's body hit the floor Ed had put two .44 Colt shells into the old man. His frail-boned body was flung back hard against the counter, blood spreading in a damp dark stain on the front of his fancy lace-collared white shirt as he slid to the floor in a crumpled heap. The mad-eyed gun crazy Ed swung his gun on to the bank manager, standing still with his arms raised high and a desperate, pleading look on his face. Ed shot him in the head. The third man to die in as many seconds in what he had believed would be an easy money raid.

Ed heard the girl give out an hysterical shriek and drop down out of sight behind the bank counter. He cursed wildly. Now there was no one to draw the bolts on the narrow iron gate at the end of the counter that would have allowed him and Bob access to the tempting open safe and its contents. His well-planned raid had turned into one bloody balls-up. It was time for the gang to high-tail it out of town. Getting shot at by irate citizens loaded down with the bank's cash was a natural risk any of the gang would take, and had taken on many a raid, but getting themselves shot for damn all was crazy business.

Ed heard footsteps behind him and spun round snarling like a cornered wolf, and almost shot Lester.

'I heard — ' Lester began then broke off on seeing the two bodies on the floor. 'Jesus Christ! he breathed.

'Let's get to hell outa here, Lester!' Ed said. 'Things ain't worked out right. We can't do anything for Bob. That old bastard lyin' alongside him shot him dead.'

Both of them came out of the bank at a rush, pausing momentarily on the porch to cast anxious glances up and down Main Street. All seemed quiet.

But Ed knew that if the men of the town hadn't the urge to risk their lives to prevent the town's bank from being robbed the marshal must have heard the shots and got up off his ass and would be haring along the street with his deputy at any moment, loaded for bear.

The marshal had been sitting on the crapper and was just slipping his suspenders over his shoulders when he heard the shooting. He ran across the few yards to the back door of his office, paused in there long enough to stuff a pistol into the top of his pants, grab a shotgun from the gun rack and knock his dozing deputy's feet off the desk with a curt, 'Move ass, Lonnie, there's shootin' trouble up at the bank.'

Milt and Bud, closer to the street, heard the faint cracks of pistol fire. 'It look's like Ed ain't gettin' it all his own way, Bud,' he said softly.

He looked at the genuine customers in the bar but saw nothing in their manner to alarm him, yet. He caught

Saul's eye and gave him a slight get-ready nod. Saul got the warning message and dug Charlie in the ribs then both of them turned round from the bar to face the drinkers at the tables, fingers twitching nervously close to their pistol butts.

Milt was rapidly getting a strong gut-feeling that the gang was losing control of the situation and that things would have to be played as and when they came. He saw the marshal and his deputy come rushing out of the jailhouse. It was time for him to back up Ed and Bob at the bank. He smashed the bar window with the barrel of his pistol, aimed it, and fired off the six loads in one non-stop rapid burst, bringing down the two lawmen in a stumbling leg-twisting fall like running hares caught by a shotgun blast.

He heard the clatter of upturned chairs behind him as the alarmed drinkers leapt to their feet, hands reaching for their guns. Saul and Charlie's pistols stayed their hands and held them where they stood.

Milt gave them a savage-eyed glare as he drew out his other pistol. 'Kill any of them who fancies himself as a hero, Saul,' he said. 'Me and Bud will go along to the bank to see how Ed's makin' out.' He favoured Saul with an icy grin. 'The local law's past botherin' us.'

Before Milt reached out to push the bar doors open, a tricky situation had turned into a real bad one for the Ed Megan gang. The man Milt had forgotten all about, the barkeep, played things his way. Face showing no emotion he put out his hand and gripped the double-barrelled sawn-off shotgun lying on a shelf under the bar counter and pulled back both triggers.

The double blast rattled the bottles and glasses on the bar shelves and blew out a section of the front of the bar. The deadly hail and splinters of wood tore into Saul and Charlie's lower backs, bending them backwards at the knees in their dying agonies. The frozen tableau of drinkers broke up and dived for cover. And Milt knew for sure that the gang had lost all their edge when shells chipped the door posts and whizzed past his ears as he flung himself through the door.

Bob, close on his heels, wasn't so lucky. Shells raised little spurts of dust on the back of his coat and he managed two more steps before he lost all use of his legs and folding in the middle, fell off the board-walk and on to the street, a dead man.

Milt would have caught up with Bud on the road to hell if Ed and Lester hadn't drawn up their horses outside the saloon and began firing through the doorway and windows. The shooting from inside ceased long enough for Milt to get clear and leap on to his mount.

'Let's go!' a grim-faced Ed shouted. 'We ain't about to rob a bank today!' He dug his heels savagely into his horse's flanks.

Milt and Lester, kick-starting their horses in a dust-raising, mad-ass gallop, followed in Ed's wake, keeping low in their saddles to dodge the wild shots from the men who had dashed out of the saloon. Ill-luck had not yet finished with the Ed Megan gang: a store owner stepped out on to his porch as the three raiders thundered past. He aimed his rifle and with one killing shot knocked Lester clear out of his saddle.

'It looks like Ed and Milt comin' in, boys,' said Cass, one of the men at the bridge. 'And they're in one helluva hurry. Those shots we heard could have been trouble. We better get ready to meet it.'

The bridge detail were up on their feet, rifles held ready, when Ed and Milt's horses came to a dust-sliding halt beside them. Cass wanted to ask Ed where the rest of the boys were but Ed had a wild-eyed look that frightened the crap out of him so he kept his mouth shut and accepted the upsetting fact that there would be no divvying up of the takings from the bank.

'Get mounted up!' Ed grated angrily.

'Once the bastards have finished countin' how many bank robbers they've downed, they'll come chasin' after us! Let's get holed-up some place and discuss whether or not it's a wise decision to try raidin' in Texas.'

8

Joel had never known better days. He felt he had lived in Little Springs all his life. Since the saving of Marshal Tweedy's life, then, when the news came into town of how he had, single-handed, prevented the blood-thirsty Comanche from harming Miss Kathy MacDowell it was, 'Good morning, Mr Garretson', or, 'How are you, Mr Garretson', whenever he met anyone in town. He was no longer a goddamned, talking-through-the-nose Yankee not welcome in Little Springs.

He had bought himself some new clothes and had taken to bathing and shaving more often, smelling sweeter. So much, he thought humorously, that it would fool Crowbait into thinking he had a new owner.

The height of his pleasure had come when the Widow Slatts had asked him to escort her to the church-meeting service. 'Why, ma'am, I'd be delighted,' he had said, beaming like some back-woods hick at being told by the beauty of the valley that he could walk out with her.

Joel didn't tell the widow that he had never been inside a church, a prayer meeting-house or whatever before. Religion had never come by his way. He had lived in a territory where only a fast gun or knife would keep a man alive. Praying for help was a waste of breath and time. And some of the so-called Christian men Joel knew, when fired up with trade whiskey, were capable of shooting their long-standing pards in some dispute over a woman or a horse.

The Christian teachings of 'love thy neighbour' didn't apply to the heathen Indians. And that went double for the 'Good Book'-spouting generals up there on the Little Big Horn territory whose Christian thinking was that the only good Indian was a dead one.

Joel was also pleased to see how fast his new home was being built, and much bigger than the original shack. The Slash Y man in charge of the job had told him that enlarging the shack had been on the orders of Mr McDowell himself.

'He said that you could get hitched one day, raise a family, Mr Garretson. Then you'll need the extra space,' the grinning ranch-hand said.

Then Joel had more fanciful, blood stirring thoughts towards the Widow Slatts, like walking her down the aisle as his bride. The puzzled ranch-hand wondered why the big Yankee was laughing his head off as he walked back to his horse.

9

A flat-bed wagon was drawn up outside the town's general store when Marshal Jimmy Slatts stepped out from his office to start his daily rounds. His face broke into a smile as he saw Miss Kathy McDowell stepping down from the seat. Straightening up, face rigid in the stern look of a no-nonsense peace officer, he strode across to her before she went into the store. He had to control the urge to run across the street, but it was no good putting on a show as an eagle-eyed, tight-assed lawman to impress Miss Kathy, then lose it all by acting like the love-sick kid he was.

'Good mornin', Miss Kathy,' he said, all polite and formal and touching the brim of his hat in greeting. He didn't say anything more in case he got tongue-tied being this close to the girl he spent most of the night and his idle daytime hours thinking about, a girl he knew he wouldn't get any closer to than he was right now. Miss Kathy could get any available boy in the county doing her bid if she was so inclined, knocking at her door to ask her grandpa for her hand in marriage.

'Why good morning to you, Marshal Slatts,' Kathy replied, smiling. Kathy hadn't really bothered dating boys, finding her work on the ranch occupying most of her time, feeling that it was her given task to look out for her grandpa as her father would have done if he had still been alive. She also felt that she and her grandpa working together gave them the strength to get over the terrible loss they had both suffered.

Suddenly Kathy found herself gazing at Marshal James Slatts with more than a pass-the-time-of-day look. Something strange was stirring inside her, an unusual feeling for her. A sensation that was beginning to redden her cheeks as though lashed by an icy wind. It was if she was seeing James Slatts for the first time. She was seeing a boy, no, a man who had had the true grit to face two killers, with the steady clear-eyed but serious gaze her grandpa and father had. A boy, if she desired a boyfriend, her grandpa wouldn't object to. Then Kathy asked herself how could she think such thoughts. Boyfriend! Why the handsome walking tall Marshal Slatts must have every girl in town running after him.

'I am buying some cloth from the store, Marshal Slatts,' she managed to stammer. 'It's to make some new drapes for the ranch-house windows. Your mother is riding with me to help me make them up. I'm picking her up on the way out.' She cast Jimmy a mischievous smile. 'You'll have to fix your own meals today, Marshal.' Then she turned and almost ran into the store before Marshal Slatts saw her fiery cheeks.

The ranch-hand who had been

driving the wagon gave Jimmy a lop-sided grin. 'I ain't seen Miss Kathy so flummoxed before. I figure she's took a likin' to you, Marshal.'

And Marshal Slatts could only stand there with his mouth wide open in disbelief. A rich rancher's granddaughter having good feelings towards him! He gave the ranch-hand a weak sickly grin in return and walked back to his office.

A little while later from his office window he saw her ride out of town with rolls of material laid in the wagon. She would be on her way to pick up his ma before riding on to the ranch. He noticed with grim satisfaction that as well as the driver the wagon had four rifle-armed outriders escorting it. Even this close to the Slash Y Mr McDowell was taking no chances with his granddaughter's life. Jimmy wasn't sure but he thought Miss Kathy looked across at his office as the wagon passed by, or so he fervently believed.

Was it true what the ranch-hand had

said? Did Miss Kathy really have good feelings towards him? Or was he only ribbing him. Young Marshal Slatts gave a deep sigh. Love, or whatever it was, he was finding out was a puzzling business. Maybe Mr Garretson could advise him on suchlike confusing matters. Though the more he thought about it that didn't seem likely. The big Yankee had spent most of his life trapping, scouting for the blue-bellies and preventing himself from being scalped by wild Indians, he wouldn't have found the time to have fallen in love.

★ ★ ★

Widow Slatts asked the wagon driver if he would mind pulling off the main trail as they came up to the creek. She smiled at Kathy.

'I want to see how Mr Garretson's new home is coming on.'

'I'm glad Mr Garretson is staying, Mrs Slatts,' Kathy said. 'He wasn't too keen to accept Grandpa's offer to rebuild his shack and clear up his land for saving my life. He told him that he was also keeping himself alive. We'll see to it that he gets through the winter until his land starts producing again.'

Jemima Slatts was also pleased that Mr Garretson had decided to make his home in the teritory. She had, contrary to her early fears about having a male lodger, got used to having him around the house. Somehow it gave her a comfortable feeling. Jimmy thought the world of him. And to her surprise she would be disappointed when Mr Garretson ceased being her lodger and left to live in his own place. She smiled wanly. Washing and repairing his clothes reminded her of what it was to have a man about the house again.

Joel was working on his own, stripped to the waist nailing planks on the side wall frame of the shack. He saw the Widow Slatts and Miss Kathy sitting in the wagon but didn't walk across the shallow creek to talk to them. He knew it would take the girl a long time to get over her fearful ordeal she had gone through, and seeing his bull's head tattoo again wouldn't help her to get over it any. And it embarrassed him at giving the widow another close look at his half-naked body and its many scars.

'My place will soon be finished, ladies,' Joel shouted. 'Thanks to the Slash Y boys, Miss Kathy. Then I'll have to have a grand house-warmin' shindig. Though you good ladies will have to do the cookin'.' Joel grinned. 'What I'd put in the cookin' pot is only fit for we old mountain men to eat.'

'We'll see to the vittles, Mr Garretson, won't we, Kathy?' Jemima called back. 'Just name the opening day! I'm going on to the Slash Y, Mr Garretson, so I won't be back home until sometime tomorrow.' Jemima smiled. 'You had better let Jimmy do the cooking, I don't want my pans ruined.'

Joel didn't start work until he could no longer see the wagon, wondering why the heck had he been so crazy living and killing like some wild critter when he could have lived in a house, slept in a soft bed along-side a fine woman the like of Widow Slatts, and raised a family that would look after their old pa. All he had to show for the life he had lived was his old trail buddy, Crowbait, who was as crazy as he was.

10

Carlos eyed the wagon bouncing along the trail. It was the two women who were passengers in it that had attracted his attention. Especially the younger one, the one whose long yellow hair was blowing loosely in the wind. Carlos drew in his breath with a gasp. Taking her was a prize worth riding into Texas for. Once he had broken her spirit she would provide him with many months of pleasure. When she ceased to inflame his blood he would sell her, for many ponies, to Red Dog, a Comanche chief who regularly visited his stronghold.

Carlos had crossed into Texas with practically the whole of his war band, his plan to lead them in one sweeping, non-stop raid then ride back across the border before the Texas Rangers could pick up their trail.

So far his plan had worked without a

hitch. Three gringo ranches had been raided and along with the many horses and what valuables there had been in the ranch houses, women and children had been taken. The horses and the captives were on their way back to the stronghold guarded by half of his *muchachos*. He had been ready to give the order for the last raid, a small ranch which would yield twenty or so horses when they saw the wagon and its escort come into view. That, reasoned Carlos, the young, a virgin he believed, must be the daughter of a gringo with standing in this part of Texas. And the older woman was not without her blood-stirring qualities.

Carlos's gold-capped teeth glinted in what passed for a smile on the death's-head mask of a face. He had never had the pleasure of deflowering a high-born gringo virgin before. He gave Antonio, his second-in-command, a burning-eyed look.

'You are about to have a fine-looking

gringo señora sharing your bed, Antonio.'

Antonio's grin was as red-eyed as his *patron*'s.

The wagon was only an hour's ride from the Slash Y range and the escort were riding at ease. The wagon driver, reins resting on his knees, was rolling a makings. Kathy and Mrs Slatts were discussing the fitting of the new drapes. Then, as though coming from hell, the earth devils came thundering out of the washes and gullies on either side of the trail, yelling like full-blood Indians and dealing out death.

The first man to die was the driver. He gasped with pain and slomped across Kathy's knees. She looked with horror at the gaping, blood-streaming hole in his side in the split-second of time before the wagon was surrounded by howling *comancheros* and the trail echoed with the sound of gunfire.

The escort were swept off their horses before they could lay their hands on their own guns by a deadly whirlwind of lead. Fear-stricken Kathy and Mrs Slatts clung to each other for mutual comfort and strength as the raiders closed in on the wagon. Mrs Slatts had never seen such evil-faced men before. Kathy had: the Comanche war band she and Mr Garretson had met up with. This time there was no Mr Garretson to save her and Mrs Slatts.

Sitting petrified with fear, they heard one of the raiders, a squat-built man whose flesh-crawling leer sent them deeper into pits of despair, shout out some orders. Then two raiders, their mounts brushing the sides of the wagon, reached over their saddles and yanked the pair, struggling and screaming, bodily off the seat. Carlos grinned at their futile efforts.

'Tie them up!' he said. 'The *señorita* will ride with me once we have taken those gringo horses, the *señora* belongs to Antonio, Pablo, so do not fondle her too much or Antonio will remove your *cajones*.' Santos's grin was wild and wide; he was in a good humour.

Kathy and Mrs Slatts were thrown roughly across the backs of the horses and their hands and feet were securely bound. Mrs Slatts, with some difficulty, was holding down the contents of her stomach as she smelt the strong, overpowering body sweat of her captor and the humiliation of the sweat-sticky probing hands squeezing her breasts and the top of her bare thighs. Dimly she heard Kathy's racking sobs as she suffered the same degrading ordeal. The terrible knowledge of what her fate would be was almost forgotten as her thoughts went out to Kathy. At least she had been taken by a gentle, loving husband in a marriage bed. The girl would lose her chastity to a fiend in human form.

The raid on the ranch was carried out just as swiftly and as bloodily as the wagon raid had been. The *comancheros* stormed in on the ranch in one howling wave, shooting dead the three gringos at the horse corral before they were able to fire a shot at their attackers.

Carlos's grin was showing again. They had taken many prizes in Texas, he would have to hold a *baile* to celebrate their successful raid. And it would be a pleasant ride back to the stronghold with a soft-fleshed *señorita* lying across his saddle.

11

Joel was on his way back to Little Springs with Crowbait strolling along at his usual leisurely pace, allowing his rider to think of what the future could hold for him. Being a sodbuster, rancher, whatever, didn't seem a wayout proposition, Joel thought. He had made friends. His old uncle had given him the chance to start a new occupation. One where he wasn't forced to eyeball every rock, patch of brush, in case there was a hostile skulking behind it ready to arrow shoot him and lift his hair. His dangerous loner days were over.

Joel's idyllic thoughts were cut short by the sound of a horse's hoofs and someone shouting out his name. He swung round in his saddle and saw a rider rein-lashing his mount coming up fast behind him. Puzzled, he drew

Crowbait to a halt.

Joel recognized the rider as one of the Slash Y crew as he stopped alongside him in a billowing cloud of dust.

'Miss Kathy and the Widow Slatts have been took by *comancheros*, Mr Garretson!' the ranch-hand gasped out. 'All the crew are out tryin' to pick up the sonsuvbitches' trail. I'm ridin' into town to ask the marshal to raise a posse to join the hunt. Though I reckon the *comancheros* will be across in New Mexico by now.'

Joel's blood chilled. 'Who are these *comancheros*?' he asked the ranch-hand.

'They're a bunch of murderin' renegades, Mr Garretson,' the rider replied. 'Mexes, 'breeds, Injuns, and white trash, the scum of the territory. They kill, rob and burn across the whole of New Mexico and as far south as old Mexico. But the bastards have never raided this far east before. They do most of their tradin' with the Comanche, horses, women and kids for the gold and other valuable pickin's the Comanche have collected in their raids. They are bossed over by a Mex who goes by the name of Carlos. I'll tell you this, Mr Garreston, *comancheros* are heap bad medicine and shootin' them dead is too good for them.'

Joel swore loud and profanely. The two females he'd developed strong feelings for in the hands of men every bit as cruel as the Sioux and the Crow warbands. He didn't have to think hard of what their fearful fate would be, if they hadn't already been raped and killed.

Face etched in hard lines he said, 'You get back and join the hunt, Mr McDowell will need every man he's got,' he said. 'I'll ride into town and get a posse raised. Then we'll ride out to the Slash Y. Ask Mr McDowell to leave a man there to tell us what section of the territory he wants us to quarter. There's no sense in checkin' ground for signs when it's already been covered.'

'Thanks, Mr Garretson,' the ranchhand said. 'The old man will be pleased. He's in one helluva state.' He yanked his horse's head round and dug his spurred boots into its ribs and with a yelled 'Yahoo!' as a further encouragement to the horse, galloped back along the trail to the Slash Y.

Before the dust of the Slash Y man's fire-balling departure had settled, Joel tugged at Crowbait's reins. 'Crowbait,' he said. 'I know you ain't got the temperament of one of those Arab full-blood stallions I once read about, old buddy, but I'm in one helluva hurry to get to Little Springs. The lives of two females are in great danger. So I would be beholden to you if you could step out kinda sharpish.' He nudged Crowbait lightly in the ribs with his heels. Crowbait took off in a leaping run that almost unseated Joel.

★ ★ ★

Joel drew up a heaving-flanked, sweat-sheening Crowbait outside the marshal's office. He swung down from his saddle

142

with a thankfully muttered, 'I'm definitely in your debt, pard, for gettin' me here in record time even though you just about bounced the balls off me.'

Crowbait gave him a foam-flecked mouth snarl of an acknowledging neigh.

Marshal Tweedy, leaning heavily on a stick, was standing in front of his desk, Deputy Slatts was sitting in the chair when Joel burst in on them.

'We need a bunch of armed men, Marshal Tweedy!' he said. 'Like right now!' Then, grim-faced, he told the peace officers about the *comanchero* raid.

A wild-eyed Jimmy leapt up from his chair. 'My ma and Miss Kathy took by *comancheros*!' he cried out, and made a dash for the door.

Joel caught him by his coat collar and held him back. 'Where the hell do you think you're goin', boy?' he said harsh-voiced.

'Why, why, I'm goin' for my horse!' Jimmy snarled, struggling to get out of Joel's tight grip. 'My ma and — '

'You're goin' off at half-cock,' interrupted Joel, voice somewhat softer in tone. 'What are you intendin' to do on your own then? Can you read sign? — if you're lucky to catch up with those *comanchero* cutthroats with that ancient six-load pistol you're kitted out with?'

'Yeah, well, but, I — ' mumbled Jimmy, calming down a little.

'I've got the same anxious feelin's for your ma and the young girl, Marshal Slatts,' Joel said. 'But we could be about to take part in a small war and we have to be prepared to wage it. Now go and get a bandoleer of reloads for your pistol and rifle, and see that your canteen's full, take an extra one, and a supply of feed for your horse. We could be days on the trail and if we get lucky and catch up with them we don't want to be short of shells, or dyin' of thirst, or ridin' a coupla horses too half-starved to break wind.' Joel gimlet-eyed Jimmy. 'You've got fifteen minutes to do all that, OK?'

Jimmy didn't answer, he was already dashing out of the office.

Joel turned and faced Marshal Tweedy. 'It's your town, Marshal, you'll know what men to pick.'

'I'll round-up some good men, Mr Garretson,' the marshal replied. 'If it wasn't that I would fall out of my saddle before we cleared the town I'd ride with you. What those sonsuvbitches could be doing to those two females has got me into a killing mood. You go and see to your own war gear; I'll have the men ready to ride out loaded for bear in the time you stipulated.'

'Thanks, Marshal,' Joel said. 'I'm a long-ways from bein' ready to fight any sort of war.' He favoured the lawman with a ghost of a smile. 'And that horse of mine will need a few sweet words in his ears. He nigh on busted a blood vessel gettin' me here; he won't be too happy knowin' his trials and tribulations ain't over yet.'

* * *

It was a posse of eight riders that pulled up outside the Slash Y big house. The grim face of the ranch-hand waiting for them to give them their orders was a clear message to Joel that there had been no good news regarding Mrs Slatts and the rancher's granddaughter.

'The crew's stretched out in one line moving west-wards towards the Pecos,' the ranch-hand told Joel. 'When we left them we'd still hadn't had any luck picking up the bastards' tracks. If we can't pick up any signs of them this side of the border, it's sure as hell we ain't goin' to get lucky in New Mexico in gettin' some idea in what direction Carlos's stronghold lies. I'll take you and your boys to Mr McDowell; he'll explain to you what section of the territory he wants you to quarter.'

⋆   ⋆   ⋆

It was a haggard-faced McDowell who greeted Joel and the men from Little Springs, a man, Joel noticed, who seemed to have aged twenty years since he had last spoken to him.

The rancher looked at Jimmy. 'Don't worry, boy,' he said. 'We'll get the pair back safe and unharmed.'

Joel knew that Mr McDowell was trying to keep the young marshal's spirits up, and his own. Tracking was a slow, painstaking business and by the distance they had travelled to get to the line of trackers, still up on their horses, Joel knew that the Slash Y men had been moving too fast and could have missed spotting any not too visible signs of the *comancheros* passing this way. Though he could understand the rancher pushing his men, every minute his granddaughter was in the hands of the *comancheros* would be another minute of hell for the old man.

'Since that business with the Comanche, Mr Garretson,' the rancher said, 'Kathy never left the ranch without a well-armed escort. There were five men with the wagon she and Mrs Slatts was travelling in. The bastards must have bushwhacked them; the boys never had a chance to fight back; they were killed to a man.' The rancher beat his saddle with his fist. 'And I didn't know damn all about it. It was one of my line riders who raised the alarm. He saw smoke rising from old man Park's property. He and his two boys run a small horse ranch on the southern edge of my land.'

Mr McDowell paused as one of his crew rode up to him to report that the small pass through the hills he had been checking out for tracks had proved negative. The rancher cursed softly, ageing still more in Joel's view. 'Join the rest of the boys then,' he told the ranch-hand. Then he faced Joel once more. 'As I said, Mr Garretson, one of my boys saw that smoke and rode over to see if Park wanted any help. Old man Park and his two sons were beyond any help. They were lying there all shot to hell and their home was burning like a furnace. And all the horses had been lifted. One of Park's boys lived long enough to tell my rider that the raiders were a mixed bunch of *hombres*, a large band, bossed by what he had heard, a Mex called Carlos. There ain't such large bands of raiders active in this part of Texas, Mr Garretson, so they must have been *comancheros*.'

Rancher McDowell, his face twisted in frustrated rage, beat at his saddle again. 'When the ranch-hand got back to the Slash Y with the news of the killings I realized that my granddaughter and Mrs Slatts could be in danger so we rode out and found the wagon and the dead men alongside it.' He kneed his mount closer to Crowbait. 'I don't want to dash the young marshal's hopes,' he said softly, 'but the sonsuvbitches have too big a lead over us and they know how to hide their tracks. Once or twice we've managed to pick up the sign of the horses they've stolen, but lost them again. I figure the band will have split up, one bunch driving the horses, the other riding fast for their hole-up with Kathy and Mrs Slatts and any other captives they've got. But, by thunder, we'll keep searching until we do cut their sign. Though I've stock to feed and water so some of the crew will have to ride back to the Slash Y. You and the men you've brought with you should fill their places.'

You won't pick up the *comancheros'* trail, Mr McDowell, not the way you're going about it, Joel thought. 'Mr McDowell,' he said 'I mean no offence, but I'm used to trackin' alone so if it's OK with you I'll set about doin' just that. Though I'll break my rule by takin' the boy with me. It'll kinda keep his mind from worryin' too much about what could be happenin' to his ma and Miss Kathy. But I'll promise you this, Mr McDowell, if I get a clear sign of the likelihood of where this Carlos is lyin' low, I'll send the boy back to the Slash Y with the news.'

'That's fine by me, Mr Garretson,' the rancher replied. 'You're the expert in such-like matters. I'll be waiting for your message.

Joel didn't have any doubts that he would find the stronghold. The sonsuvbitches weren't birds. Even Indians leave tracks if a man looked close enough to see them. But whether he would be in time to save the girl and Mrs Slatts from being used was something he wasn't prepared to commit himself.

'Marshal Slatts!' he called out. 'Let's do some trackin'!' And with a, 'Hope to have news for you soon, Mr McDowell', he cut away from the main line of searchers with Jimmy following him.

12

Jimmy Slatts thought Mr Garretson was more Indian than the genuine, copper-skinned, hair-lifting ones the way he looked for sign. The big Yankee would dismount and examine the trail with his nose only inches from the dirt as if he could smell whoever or whatever had passed by that way. However hard he looked at the same spot he couldn't see the slightest sign of tracks of any shape or size.

And for the second day since the town had been told of the fearful news of the capture of his mother and Miss Kathy McDowell by the bloodthirsty *comancheros*, Mr Garretson got to his feet after reading the trail with his face as hard-boned as an Indian's, muttering words under his breath that Jimmy took to be strong curse words.

'I'll give those sonsuvbitches credit

for one thing, boy,' Joel grated. 'They sure know how to hide their tracks. We've been informed that these *comancheros* hole-up somewhere in the north of New Mexico. I ain't been there, but I reckon it's one hell of a big place. If we can't pick up their trail where they've recrossed that river up ahead you call the Pecos, to give us a hint in which direction they're headin' in, then by heck, in spite of Mr McDowell pinnin' his hopes on me rescuing his daughter and your ma I'll have to admit I ain't up to the task.'

Seeing his young partner's disappointed look and knowing how chewed up inside he must be about the fate of his ma and the girl he had strong feelings for, he said, more confidently than he was feeling, 'But I ain't given up the task yet, Deputy. There's still several hours of daylight left and the closer we get to the Pecos these bastards we're seekin', thinkin' that they're not far from the New Mexican border, might get careless and leave a trail.'

Lack of quick, positive results had sent Jimmy's hopes nose-diving. Like rancher McDowell he'd had great faith in the old army scout and Indian fighter's ability as a tracker. After all, he had rescued Miss Kathy from the Comanche. He had blindly thought that Mr Garretson could come up with another miracle by rescuing her and his ma from the *comancheros*.

But Jimmy was growing up fast. He had taken part in a shoot-to-the-death gunfight with two border ruffians and now he was on the trail of at least twenty Mexican and 'breed killers. He was beginning to realize that Mr Garretson's successes as an army scout and his rescuing of Miss Kathy had damn all to do with miracles. It took sheer guts and a fast gun to pull through on the winning side in Mr Garretson's profession. And he had better start developing such-like quali-ties so he would be ready to back up his partner, to the death if needs be when they finally nosed them out. Though Jimmy's thoughts of only two guns against twenty didn't encourage blowhard thinking.

Jimmy's uneasy ruminations were abruptly ended as he heard Mr Garretson say sharply, 'Hold up there, Deputy, there's sign showin' here!'

Jimmy hadn't deliberately drawn out his Winchester from its boot but there it was resting across his saddle horn. So much for acquiring nerves of steel, Jimmy thought morosely. Though at least his reflexes were sharpening up. He would need hair-trigger reactions when they met up with the *comancheros*.

'Are they the tracks of the *comancheros*, Mr Garretson?' he asked.

'No, boy,' Joel replied, still bent low across his saddle eyeing the ground. 'There's only five or six riders and they ain't headin' towards the border.' He straightened up on his horse and nodded in the direction of the range of mountains. 'They're makin' for that canyon. If we don't see the same tracks comin' outa there, bein' that the sign is fresh, the fellas up on those horses must be still in there.' He looked at Jimmy. 'Take off your badge, Deputy,' he said.

'Take off my badge, why?' a puzzle-faced Jimmy replied.

'We could be ridin' into trouble,' Joel said.

'Trouble?' Jimmy croaked. His rifle moving on its own accord again was up across his chest now pointing towards the canyon entrance.

'Why would men ride into that canyon?' asked Joel. 'Are they ranch-hands takin' a short cut through the mountains to get to their spread? And, as I said, they ain't the *comancheros*.'

Jimmy's face broke into an under-standing smile. 'Why they're a bunch of owlhoots, Mr Garretson. West Texas is crawlin' with lawbreakers.'

'We're goin' into that canyon,' Joel said, 'and if those fellas are still there have words with them. They could have seen the *comancheros* hightailin' it to the border. It's a wild chance, but we ain't got any more possible leads.' He smiled thinly at Jimmy. 'They're bound to be tetchy-nerved men and sportin' a marshal's badge ain't likely to unwind them any. They're more than likely shoot the pair of us out of hand. Now we go in all smiles: we ain't seekin' trouble.' Joel hard-eyed Jimmy. 'But if it comes we'll have to meet it, fast, savvy?'

Joel saw his young partner's worried and concerned look and his gaze softened somewhat. 'You'll do OK, boy, never fear. You've handled two gunmen before.' He grinned. 'I'll take on the other three or four of the gang.'

★ ★ ★

It had been a week since the failed bank raid and a long ways from where they were holed-up, and Ed, opining that things must have quietened down in the territory, the law thinking the raiders were now in New Mexico, thought it was time the Ed Megan gang did some more raiding. He was lucky he still had a gang, albeit only half the strength of what it was when they crossed into Texas. Ed had expected Cass and the other three Texas boys after the balls-up of a raid to quit the gang and ride back to the Panhadle and take up ranch work to tide them over.

'Now you Texicans can pull out,' he had told them. 'You lost some good buddies back there in that town for no recompense. You boys are young enough to take up an honest trade. Me and Milt are too old to change our ways; we've been on the run since the end of the war with prices on our heads.' Ed thin-smiled. 'We m'be couldn't tackle a bank heist but the two of us could hold-up a stage or a suttler's store.'

'We Texicans ain't quiters, Ed,' Cass replied with some force in his voice. 'The gang's done OK since it was formed. Even in a regular job you're bound to get a off day sometimes. We'll stay; that's the way we want it, boys, isn't it?' Cass got asserting nods from the three other Texans.

Ed's hard face cracked in a genuine smile. 'Boys, you're more than welcome to stay.'

Ed had come to the decision to lead the gang south along the Pecos. There was bound to be a ranch, a settlement, even a small town along the east bank. Whatever showed up first and if it looked worthwhile to raid, they would hit it in the old way, a quick guerilla-like strike. Grab what could be taken then ass-kick it across the line into New Mexico to set up their deal with Carlos again.

He got up on to his feet and walked across to the Texans sitting at the camp-fire to put the plan to them for them to OK it. Milt, on watch at the mouth of the canyon, would need no convincing. He stopped suddenly when he saw Milt come hurrying round the dog-leg bend in the canyon. There was a cursing at the fire as the Texans leapt to their feet and grabbed for their rifles at Milt's shouted warning of, 'Two riders comin' in!'

Ed picked up his own rifle. 'The law?' he asked as Milt came up to him.

Milt shook his head. 'It looks like an old saddletramp and a young kid, Ed. And there ain't anyone tailin' them. So there ain't any need for gun play, not straight away. They could tell us what's goin' on in the territory they've passed through.'

'Why the hell are they ridin' into this particular canyon, Ed?' Cass said.

Ed gave him a wolfish grin. 'That's one of the first questions I intend puttin' to them, Cass.'

Joel, in the lead, first saw the group of men standing at the fire holding their rifles as he swung round the bend in the trail. In two seconds flat he knew that he had surmised right the trade of the men whose horse tracks he had seen, anything that wasn't honest-raised sweat toil. He had seen more charitable-looking Sioux all painted up for a white-eye killing spree.

'Crowbait,' he said softly. 'Those

gents up ahead are one of the meanest bunch of takin' men I've ever had the misfortune to clap eyes on. We're ridin' into one helluva situation here. I'm truly sorry I brung the kid in with me.'

Joel drew Crowbait back slightly until an apprehensive-looking Jimmy came up alongside him.

'You do nothin', boy, but look happy,' he growled. 'Let me do all the talkin'. And for Chris' sake don't even glance at your guns. Savvy?'

A dry-throated Jimmy, eyeing the welcome committee in front of him, could only nod that he savvied.

Ed gave the older rider, a man as tall as he was, but nowhere as bulky, wearing a long coat, a close-eyed look. Then took in the nervous-looking boy. He opined that Milt's reading of them had been right, the two didn't have the cut of badge-toting lawmen, or bounty hunters either. As the pair came in close, he was just as sure Milt had been amiss to catalogue them as a couple of saddle-tramps, drifters. The older man, up on a freak of a horse, and smiling fit to burst had the sharp-eyed gaze of a man who knew what he was about, a man who couldn't be intimidated in any way. Ed gripped his rifle that much tighter; he wasn't used to be stared down.

Joel opened up the talking, putting all his cards on the table. He nodded a greeting to the burly, black-whiskered man whom he guessed was the boss of the bunch.

'Pilgrim,' he said, 'I ain't a mealy-mouthed gabbler so I'll tell you why I rode in here, I'm here to seek information.' His skin-deep smile widened. 'Now I ain't as dumb to think that me and the boy have rode into a Bible-salesmen's conference, but how you earn your wherewithal ain't any concern of mine. I — '

'You're a goddamned Yankee, ain't you, Pilgrim?' interrupted Milt. 'I rate them lower than Injuns.'

Joel sensed the rising tension of the men at the fire. He cursed under his breath. Outnumbered by a bunch of owlhoots was bad enough, when they were also Yankee-haters didn't improve the odds of him and the kid riding out of the canyon sitting upright on their horses. It was win-or-lose time. In spite of his fears it was time for tough talking.

Joel's face stoned over and he eyeballed the Yankee-hater. 'Yes I am, Reb, but this Yankee is tryin' to track down a band of cut-throat renegades who call themselves *comancheros* to try and rescue a young Texas girl and my young pard's ma the sonsuvbitches have took! Now, bein' a goddamned Yankee, I ain't qualified to comment on the response of a Texan on hearing that two of his womenfolk are in the hands of such-like scum. But I'll tell you this, mister, in Montana, where I hail from, even the town's dogs would join in the hunt if some females of ours were took by the Sioux.'

Then Joel did some quick mental calculations as he wondered if he would have the time to yank out the double-barrelled shotgun stuck in his bedroll and blow to hell maybe two, three of the owlhoots before they cut down him and kid with their rifles.

It was Cass who retaliated against Joel's insult. 'Why you horse-faced, Yankee sonuvabitch!' he cried. 'We Texans — !'

Ed cut off his angry tirade with a snapped, 'Calm down, Cass!'

Ed gave Joel a fish-eyed look. 'Are you sure it was *comancheros* who took those females you spoke of? They weren't Injuns, Comanche, Utes, Apache?'

'We're sure, mister.' Jimmy's voice was only a hoarse whisper.

'My pard's right,' Joel said. 'And I have been told the bastards hole-up someplace across there in New Mexico. We've been quarterin' the territory for days and we ain't even got a whiff of their trail. And other men are out searchin' as well, with the same goddamned luck. My last hope was to nose along the Pecos to see if I can pick up their sign where they forded the river. Then I spotted your tracks.' Joel paused long enough to smile at the burly man. 'For men who seem to have a pressing need to lie low for a spell, you didn't make a good job of coverin' out your tracks. We came in here on the off chance that you had seen a big bunch of riders, or their dust trail, headin' for the New Mexican border. M'be point me in a more particular direction of their whereabouts than I know right now.'

'It's that bastard Carlos's doin', Ed,' Milt said. 'Him and his boys musta followed us into Texas.'

Carlos? Joel pricked up his ears. They could be getting their first break. He had heard the name of the boss man of the group they were trailing. These men he was talking to must have had dealings with the *comancheros*. Which was only natural, he thought. They were bandits all and it would be in their best thieving interests to exchange information such as the best ranch to rob or where the law was operating in the territory.

'We can't let those greaser bastards get away with takin' our women,' Cass said angrily.

Joel noted with some satisfaction it was the Yankee-hater who had spoken. He had an ally of sorts.

'Cass's right,' Milt added. 'Why Bob would spin round in his grave if he thought that some Mex, or Injun, was having his way with some southern women.'

Joel relaxed somewhat in his saddle. The threat of him and the boy being shot had receded. Now it was up to the mean-eyed Ed, the gang's boss, to say his part on the issue.

Ed was doing some thinking between dirty-mouthing Carlos. Milt was right, the greaser son-of-a-bitch had sneaked into Texas to do some raiding of his own while the law was busy hunting down a bunch of would-be bank robbers, the Ed Megan gang. He cast another assaying glance at the tall Yankee and still couldn't figure out what trade he followed. He could, he opined, have once worn a marshal's badge, or equally been a hold-up man like himself. In spite of his doubts he didn't believe the tale he had told him about the women being captured by Carlos wasn't the truth. He held no owlhoot loyalty towards Carlos, a man he knew would have sold them out to the lawmen if it suited his purpose.

'You're right, mister,' he said. 'About those *comancheros* holed up in New Mexico.' He favoured Joel with a cold grin. 'Though you must have a mite of Injun blood in you to have picked up our sign, you'll never find Carlos's stronghold. But if you do kinda accidentally stumble across it, you'll never be able to get those females you spoke of out of the camp. Carlos has a whole army of Mex, 'breeds, and renegade whites holed up with him. It so happens me and my boys are headin' back to New Mexico and if you are willin' we'll take you right to Carlos's front door.'

'Why that's mighty obligin' of you, mister,' replied Joel. 'As for gettin' the women out, I'll play it as it comes.'

'But we'll ride ahead of you and the kid,' Ed said, set-faced. 'If you're seen in our company by a marshal's posse, bein' that illegal Bible sellin' is against the law in Texas, you'll get shot at like the rest of us. Once we've crossed the New Mexican line we'll join up with you again, OK?'

'That's fine by me, friend,' replied Joel. 'Me and my pard were beginnin' to lose hope in findin' the hole-up so we'll do what you think is best. We'll stay here to feed and water our horses so that oughta allow you to get well ahead of us. You pick us up when it's safe for you and your boys to show your faces.'

★   ★   ★

'Are we going to let Mr McDowell know we've got a lead right into Carlos's camp, Mr Garretson?' Jimmy asked when they were ready to ride out.

'We can't, boy,' Joel said. 'We ain't got a lovin' relationship with those owlhoots, so if we meet up with them again and we've got a bunch of riders taggin' along with us, they'll think we've sold them out and brung a marshal's posse to rope them in. And bang goes our way into Carlos's camp. And shootin' our way into the place with the Slash Y crew, lookin' to spill *comanchero* blood, is a sure way to get your ma and the girl killed. It's up to you and me, boy, to get them out and I ain't about to fool you by sayin' it'll be a piece of cake. But the stakes are sure worth it.'

'Amen to that, Mr Garretson,' Jimmy said, with some fervour as he swung into his saddle.

13

Joel and Jimmy were riding due north along the west bank of the Pecos, neither of them knowing whether they were still on Texas soil or had crossed the New Mexican border. Or riding in the direction the *comancheros* had taken. Only the 'Bible sellers' could tell them that, Joel thought sourly. When the bastards showed themselves, that is.

Joel believed they were roughly following the *comancheros*' trail though as yet he hadn't seen any sighting of it. Reasoning as a man who'd had more than often to hide his trail, he didn't doubt that the raiders would use the Pecos as much as they could to cover their tracks, riding in the river where it was shallow and coming out on dry land where the ground was too hard and stony to show up any tracks.

But Joel knew they were travelling

too damn slow. What pain, fear and indignities the Widow Slatts and the young girl must be suffering had built up a cold hatred inside him against the *comancheros*. It was a deep hate that he had never felt against his old enemies, the Sioux, the Crow and the Cheyenne, men who had been trying to kill him for years. Up there in the high country it had only been him and and the hostiles fighting under the basic rule of kill or be killed. If he had ended up dead, well, that would have been the luck of the draw.

Now he was finding out what it was like to have strong feelings for someone who was in great danger. He had never possessed the killing lust, only killing to protect himself or his partners. But he had it now. He would kill every son-of-a-bitch who stood between him and the Widow Slatts and Miss Kathy and enjoy doing it.

Jimmy was having similar worrying thoughts and had the need to ask Mr Garretson how he rated their chances of rescuing his ma and Miss Kathy, but was too scared to ask him on seeing the fierce-eyed look his gaunt-faced partner had.

'There's our 'friends' up ahead, Mr Garretson,' Joel heard Jimmy say.

He lifted his head and saw the owlhoots and his spirits lightened somewhat. They wouldn't be stumbling all over New Mexico, if the boss of the gang kept his word. He gave them a curt nod as he and Jimmy drew up beside them.

'Friend,' Joel said to Ed. 'I know I ain't in a position to bargain with you, but I'd be right obliged if you'd hold to your promise of taking us to Carlos's hideout with some haste.'

Ed gave him a long eyeballing before he spoke. 'You know what you and the kid are letting yourselves in for paying a visit to that hell's kitchen, Yankee?'

Joel favoured Ed with a slow spreading, all-toothed smile that in no way softened his look. 'It's what the comancheros have let themselves in for, friend, for capturing two Texan ladies. I have a great urge to shed *comanchero* blood. M'be get so het up as to lift their hair, Injun style.'

Ed was a hard man. He had ridden alongside equally hard men, Quantrill, Jesse and Frank James, the Younger boys, real taking men all his life, but the tall horse-faced Yankee beat them all. The long-faced bastard was making him feel uncomfortable. Stick a couple of feathers in his hair, Ed opined, take off his shirt and put a hatchet in his hand and he could be gazing at a bronco Indian in all but colour.

'I gave you my word, 'friend',' he said. 'I'll take you to Carlos's hole-up. It just kinda took me back somewhat meeting a man, even a Yankee, so keen on committing suicide.'

'Let's go then,' Joel replied. He smiled. 'Just to ease your mind, me and the boy already know we're a couple of crazy-minded fellas.'

'Company comin' in, Ed,' Cass said suddenly.

Ed swung round and narrow-eyed the eight or nine riders trotting along the trail towards them. 'Smells like a bunch of lawmen to me, Cass,' Ed growled, and reached for his pistol. Then there was a general movement from the gang to reach for rifles and pistols.

Joel cursed. In another minute or two all hell was going to break loose here, and his only lead to Carlos's stronghold would be gone in a welter of blood. Though, on reflection, that wouldn't matter, as more than likely he and his partner would be killed alongside the outlaws. He could talk himself out of this hairy situation, but Ed and his boys were not the talking kind. Gunfire stated their case. As soon as the riders came in close, lawmen or not, Ed would open up the deadly talking. To Joel's surprise it was his young partner who tried to cool things down.

'You fellas stay your hands,' Jimmy said with a strength of authority in his voice that surprised, and pleased Joel.

'There ain't any need for gunplay.' He nudged his horse past the outlaws to meet the incoming riders. And, most unusual for Jimmy, dirty-mouthing under his breath as he did so.

Jimmy was sweating blood. He was taking one hell of a chance banking on an out-and-out bad-ass taking the word of a wet-behind-the-ears kid. Any moment he expected Ed to put a bullet in his back. But it was a gamble he had to take otherwise the attempted rescue of his ma and Miss Kathy would end right here.

Ed gave Joel a what-the-hell look. 'What's the kid up to, Yankee?' he asked.

'He's tryin' to save us all from bein' shot down,' replied Joel. 'That kid, believe it or not, is a bona-fide peace officer. But don't fret any, he ain't about to turn you all in. He's got too much at stake to do that. Trust him.' He grinned at the scowling-faced Ed. 'I figure you're kinda upset inside knowin' you've been on talkin' terms with a town marshal.'

Ed took a long look at Joel then some of the tension and alarm faded from his face. 'OK, boys,' he said reluctantly. 'Do as the kid said. It ain't as though we're holding the winning hand here.'

Jimmy, openly showing his badge on his shirt, rode right up to the riders, and saw it was a posse; the leading rider, an elderly man, had a State Marshal's badge clipped to his vest. 'Howdy, Marshal,' he said all smiles. 'I'm Marshal Slatts of Little Springs across the line in Texas. Mr Tweedy, the town's regular marshal got himself shot up in a brush with two robbers, I'm standing in for him until he's fit for duty again.'

State Marshal Grover, old enough to have been Jimmy's grandpappy, gave him a jaundiced-eyed glare. 'You're a long ways out of your jurisdiction, temporary Marshal Slatts, ain't you?' He nodded in the direction of the outlaws. 'And I take it those *hombres* are your deputies?'

'Sort of,' replied Jimmy.

Marshal Grover's eyebrows rose sharply. 'Sort of!' he gasped. 'And of what purpose would a Texas peace officer with a 'sorta' bunch of deputies be doing here in New Mexico?'

'Why, we're here trying to track down a band of *comancheros* bossed over by a cutthroat called Carlos,' Jimmy said angrily, getting his dander up at the down-putting attitude of the marshal. 'The sonsuvbitches raided Mr McDowell's ranch and took his granddaughter, and my ma, as prisoners! Ain't that a damn good reason for us to be in New Mexico, Marshal? Those men are some of the crew of the Slash Y,' he lied. 'The tall fella is an ex-army scout from Montana, he's our guide.' Jimmy gave the old lawman an admonishing look. 'Haven't the local law hereabouts been notified by wire of the raid?'

'Yeah, the Texas Rangers have wired the border lawmen about the raid,' the marshal admitted with some respect in his voice, feeling that the young Texan had well and truly taken him down a peg or two. 'But Carlos and the scum he leads are regular will 'o the wisps. We know their hole-up is somewhere in the Llana Estacado but that's thousands of square miles of damn all and crawling with other bad-asses. I hope that Yankee is a good tracker; he'll need to be. Me and my men are doing some tracking of our own. We're trying to round up a band of agency-jumping Comanche who are having themselves a burning and killing spree. So, and this is in no way belittling your problem, Marshal, I've kinda got my hands too full at present to be able to give you any assistance in your hunt for Carlos, but I will have a word or two with your Yankee tracker. Tell him some of the places where he needn't bother to look for Carlos. Could save your men and their horses some unnecessary sweat.'

Jimmy got hot again. If Ed and his gang had their likenesses posted, the marshal would recognize them. And he and Mr Garretson would be back in the middle of a more than likely shoot-out again.

Then luck swung Jimmy's way. A rider came racing up to the posse and pulled up his mount at the side of the marshal. 'Me and Joe have picked up the red devils' trail, Marshal!' the rider said. 'It's a hot one! They can't be more than an hour or so ahead of us. Joe's still trackin' them.'

'Good!' Marshal Grover snapped. Then, raising his voice, added, 'Sharpen up, men, we're back in business!' He looked at Jimmy. 'I reckon I'll have to put off that talk with your scout, Marshal, but good luck in your hunt for Carlos and I hope you get your womenfolk back unharmed. OK, men let's move out!' In a flurry of kicked-up dust, the posse cut off from the trail to ride westwards.

Joel noticed that the kid's face had hardened up into strong resolute lines as he rode back to them. In the last few minutes his partner had changed from a boy into a man. He hoped he would have a long and worthwhile manhood.

'It was a marshal's posse, Mr Garretson,' Jimmy said. 'The marshal knew about the raid, but he had seen no sign of the comancheros. They can't help us because they're in hot pursuit of a bunch of bronco Indians.' Jimmy looked Ed full in the eyes, confident he had the balls to stand up to him, hard-bitten law-breaker or not, and to face him man to man if ever that situation ever came about. 'I told you there would be no need for gunplay, I explained to the marshal that you and your boys were Slash Y hands.'

Ed, no longer trigger-fingered and suspicious-eyed, watched the posse disappear in the heat-haze before speaking. 'So you did, Marshal, so you did.' He grinned at Jimmy. 'But men in my business tend to get nervous within gunshot of lawmen.'

'Now your delicate nerves have settled down, Ed,' Joel said, 'we can get on with the task we came here for. Time ain't on our side.'

'Yankee,' Ed said. 'I said I would take you to Carlos's hole-up, but seeing your smooth-talking pard has just got me and my boys out of a real tight situation, I'll take you right inside the camp. You passed us off as ranch-hands, Marshal; I'll pass you off as two new members of my gang. That's if you don't mind riding in with wanted men.'

'I'll ride in with Old Nick himself if it will aid me to rescue my ma and Miss Kathy,' replied Jimmy.

Ed shot a glance at his men to see if there was any disagreement among them about his decision.

'You'll get no argument from me or the boys on that score, Ed,' Cass said. 'Besides, I've a hankerin' to push a sharp stick up Carlos's nose. Takin' those ladies off him will sure do that.'

Joel grinned at Jimmy. 'It ain't been such a wild idea after all tryin' to rescue the women, Marshal,' he said. 'If our luck still holds, Carlos is in for one big unpleasant surprise. OK, Ed, let's go, you're the boss from now on in.'

* * *

They had been riding at a steady pace for more than four hours, the trail twisting and turning this way and that, under beetle-browed rocky bluffs and across treeless, barren flatlands. But always veering north. Without the outlaws leading them, Joel knew that his and the kid's chances of effecting a rescue would have only been wishful dreams. The Llana Estacado was as wild and trackless a piece of territory he had ever travelled over.

At one of their regular halts to ease their and their mounts' backs, Cass said that his horse had picked up a stone in one of its front legs and was walking lame and that he wouldn't be able to keep up with them.

Ed looked up at the sky then at Joel. 'I know you're keen to get to the camp, Yankee, but with Cass's horse slowing us down we won't make it until well after dark. And riding unannounced into Carlos's stronghold in the dark ain't an advisable thing to do, if we all want to stay alive. There's a settlement a coupla miles ahead of us; we can spend the night there and see to Cass's horse.'

'That's OK by me,' replied Joel. 'As I said you're the boss of the outfit.'

The settlement consisted of a couple of dozen timber and adobe buildings and several patches of growing land scattered around a larger building that stood on its own. Joel couldn't see any of its inhabitants, even the children whom he thought would have been playing outside their houses.

'There must be some *comancheros* here, Yankee,' Ed said, guessing what was passing through Joel's mind. 'Those sonsuvbitches tend to throw a scare in God-fearing families, especially those who have pretty young daughters.'

As the party swung round one end of

the big building, Joel saw two horses tethered out front.

'There, what did I tell you, Yankee,' Ed said. 'Carlos regularly sends his men into the settlements just to check out if any *rurales* are prowling around. Sometimes the *muchachos* come in to have their way with a village girl for free. We'll go into the cantina and make our presence known here.'

Several flickering-flamed storm lanterns provided the only light in the cantina, hardly holding back the darkness of the oncoming night. The few tables and chairs in front of the planks-on-barrel-tops bar were unoccupied. The barkeep, a pot-bellied old man, stood behind the bar, idly polishing a glass. The owners of the two horses, small, thick-built, bowlegged men, were drinking at the bar. With a jangle of heavy spurs they turned to face the newcomers and Joel saw that they were both Mexicans with faces as cruel and mean-looking as any he had gazed at in his hazardous life as a scout and trapper.

'Why it's our amigo, Señor Megan!' one of the Mexicans said smiling. 'Did you get much gold in Texas?' His cold-eyed look swept over Joel and Jimmy. 'And you have new *compadres* riding with you.'

'Yeah, that I have, amigo,' Ed said. 'I lost some good boys in Texas for no gold at all. I'm hopin' to renew our old business with Carlos again.'

Over the years Joel had developed a feeling for danger before it came up and hit him. He was getting that feeling now. The Mexican's smile had slipped for a moment as he glanced at Jimmy. It had only been a skin deep sort of a smile, but the alarmed look in his eyes Joel knew was for real. Joel saw him pass that look to his partner before he invited them all to step up to the bar and have the drinks on him.

'Ed,' he said low-voiced, 'those two ugly-faced amigos of yours know we're not what we seem to be. I don't know how, but they're mighty suspicious of us. They can't be allowed to ride outa here to tell Carlos what they suspect, or we're as good as dead when we ride into that stronghold.'

'Are you sure, Yankee?' Ed asked close-eyeing Joel. 'You ain't just getting a mite nervous now we're getting close to Carlos's camp.'

'No it ain't that, I — ' Joel stopped speaking. He had caught a glimpse of metal beneath Jimmy's coat as he bellied up to the bar. He cursed softly. 'The fool kid is sporting his marshal's badge. He must have worn it when he parlayed with that posse and forgot to remove it.'

Ed did some cursing of his own and his hand dropped on to his pistol. Joel reached out and held his hand.

'No shootin',' he warned. 'Gunfire will attract attention and let the villagers know that a bunch of gringos have killed two of Carlos's men. How long can that news be kept from Carlos, eh? Let those two make their first move;

it won't be long before they do; they'll be eager to tell their boss that his gringo tradin' pards are in cahoots with the law.'

'Have you got a plan to stop the bastards from leaving, Yankee?' Ed asked.

'I'm workin' hard on one,' replied Joel, his eyes still fixed on the two *comancheros*.

After about a half-hour of downing tequilas, one of the Mexicans, smiling as though he was enjoying drinking with the gringos, said it was time that he and his *compadre* were riding back to their camp. Grinning lewdly, he said, 'Our women will be waiting for us, amigos. I will tell Carlos that his gringo *compadres* will soon be riding in.'

I bet you will, Ed thought. So the greaser sonuvabitch can be ready to gun us down. Aloud he said, smiling as falsely, 'Yeah, you do that, friend. And pick out some hot-blooded females for me and my boys to enjoy. That side of our lives has been kinda neglected lately.'

After much back-slapping and parting 'Adios amigos', the pair made their way to the door. Joel inclined his head slightly at Ed and followed them out, Ed trailing in his wake wondering how the Yankee was going to play it to stop them from riding out. He was soon to find out and it happened so quickly he almost missed it.

With a final, 'Adios amigos', one of the Mexicans put his left foot into his stirrup prior to swinging himself into the saddle, his back towards Joel. Joel put an arm under his chin and jerked back his head. His right hand, holding the knife, moved fast. And Ed caught a fleeting sight of steel as the knife slashed across the Mexican's throat. Before his body slumped to the dirt, Joel lunged at the dead man's compadre, burying the knife hilt deep between his ribs. A killing thrust that dropped him to the ground, to lie there, limbs twitching for the last few seconds he had yet to live.

'Jesus Christ!' Ed breathed. 'Where

the hell did you learn to kill like that, Yankee?'

Joel bent down, wiping the blood off his knife on one of the Mexicans' coats, looked up at Ed. His smile was as cold-looking as his knife's blade. 'From wild fellas the French trappers called the throat slitters. We Yankees know them as the Sioux.' He stood up and sheathed his knife. 'Now we've got to get rid of them and hide the horses well away from here. We don't want any other *comanchero* stumblin' over their bodies while we're in the camp. Though what I hope to do there has to been done quickly. As I said, time ain't on me and the kid's side.'

'I'll get a couple of the boys to help us,' Ed said.

'We'll do the job ourselves,' replied Joel. 'We don't want to arouse the barkeep's suspicions by goin' in and draggin' some of your men away from the bar; he could have flappin' ears and hear what he shouldn't. And bein' this close to Carlos's stronghold he'll want to keep in the bastard's favour and could pass the news of the sudden disappearance of two of his men.'

'That makes sense, Yankee,' Ed said. 'I take it you'll tell the kid to hide his badge from now on in.' He thin smiled. 'You can't slit a whole campful of throats as slick as you are in the practice.'

'I'll tell him all right, you can bet on it,' said Joel.

★　★　★

It was a low-spirited and chastened-looking Jimmy who rode out of the settlement just after dawn. That his foolishness could have got them all killed had damped down his new found confidence and pride. He wasn't so sure now that he could stand firm alongside Mr Garretson come what may.

'We were lucky this time,' Joel had told him. 'If I'd missed that Mexican's look and hadn't the chance to kill him and his buddy we could all have been ridin' into a trap. When we ride into that stronghold we can't rely on luck pullin' us through. It will take quick, real thinkin' work; we won't be able to have a second chance at rescuing your ma. One mistake and we're dead. Understand?'

A blood-drained-faced Jimmy nodded. Downcast-eyed he said, 'What about Ed and his gang, Mr Garretson? What do they think of my stupidity?'

'Only me and Ed are privy to it, kid,' Joel said. 'So it's history. It's how you act in the future that matters now.' He didn't let Jimmy know that Ed hadn't told his men about the badge incident in case they wouldn't want to ride with a kid whose carelessness could have got them killed. Seeing Jimmy was almost in tears he said, 'You'll do OK, Marshal Slatts. You ain't the only fella to have made a mistake, I've made scores and I'm still here. You learn from your mistakes or die.'

A little colour came back into Jimmy's cheeks and he straightened up in his saddle. He had to get a grip of himself if he wanted to be able to help rescue his ma and Miss Kathy.

Joel caught up with Megan riding at the head of the small column. 'The kid's feelin' sorry for himself right now,' he said, 'but I'm willin' to trust him to watch my back if things go wrong.'

Ed gave a non-committal grunt. 'We'll only find out if the kid's got balls when that happens. Then it will be too late to do anything about it.'

'What about you and your boys, Ed?' Joel said. 'You're ridin' into deep trouble. Whether or not I can sneak the women out or fight my way out, Carlos ain't goin' to be too happy towards you, not when two of your gang have stolen his women.'

'Yankee,' Ed said, 'we aim to follow in your trail dust outa that camp once you've got the females. But helping you to save those Texan females ain't the main reason I'm riding into the camp.' He gave Joel a bare-toothed grimace of a grin. 'I'm aimin' to kill Carlos. That sonuvabitch sneaked into Texas on our heels. While me and my boys, what was left of them, were sweating our balls off dodging marshals' posses, Carlos and his cutthroats were doing their own raidin'.' Ed scowled. 'Easy pickin's raidin'. Right now the bastard will be laughing fit to bust on how he used a bunch of gringo pigs to his advantage. He's made me, Ed Megan, as the Injuns put it, lose face. And a man, even an no-good owlhoot like me, has his pride.'

'I read somewhere,' Joel said, 'that great minds think along the same lines. Me and you, Ed, must have such-like head pieces because I was figurin' on pluggin' Mr Carlos for layin' his dirty hands on two people I have good feelin's for. But I ain't goin' to fight you for which of us should do the good deed.'

'That time ain't too far away, Yankee,' Ed said. 'See!' He pointed to the distant figure on a ridge to their left. 'That's the first of Carlos's lookouts.' Ed raised his right hand and gave the sentry a wave.

Joel saw the sheen of the early morning sun's rays on the guard's rifle. Warring time was here. He eased back Crowbait until his young partner caught up with him. He could keep a fatherly eye on him, Joel thought, as he had promised his ma, if the sentry decided that this was the nearest to the stronghold the gringos were going to get.

14

The Widow Slatts and Kathy McDowell had spent the best part of four days and nights locked in the shack. Painfully slow passing hours of fearful apprehension of when their horrifying thoughts became brutal reality. Bruised and aching-limbed from the ride to the camp, face down on the horses' backs, they had seen very little of their captors and the camp, having been dragged off the mounts and practically thrown into the shack. The shack, a dirty hovel of a place, had only one cot in it with a blanket that to Kathy smelt of the stables. For their toilet there was a half-filled bucket of tepid, not too clean water, then the skin-crawling embarrassment of pleading with the guard to allow them to leave the shack to relieve themselves. And the grinning guard, all eyes, escorted them to a patch of nearby brush.

Yet Jemima Slatts knew that their sufferings were nothing to the pain and mental torture they would have to face when the *comancheros*, whose horses she and Kathy had been tied to, came to have their pleasure with them.

Kathy was still in shock and had hardly spoken since they had been imprisoned in the shack. Mrs Slatts sat down on the cot next to her and, putting a comforting arm around her, drew Kathy close to her. She felt the young girl shivering and she held her tighter.

'We mustn't give up hope yet, Kathy,' she said. 'Your grandpa will have his whole crew out searching for us. They're bound to pick up the *comancheros*' trail. And I expect Mr Garretson will be with them and he's an expert tracker.' And so will Jimmy, Mrs Slatts thought. She was praying with all her soul to be saved from the terrible fate awaiting her but not at the expense of Jimmy and Mr Garretson losing their lives in the attempt. Though in reality she knew it would take a big miracle to see them rescued. In the meantime she could only comfort Kathy with lies and keep on praying that the next time the shack door opened it was the guard with their food, not the fearful sight of the chief coming for Kathy. Or the runting hog of a man who had been pawing at her thighs and breasts on the ride to the camp.

★　★　★

Joel picked out another three lookouts and opined that Carlos would have other guards out he couldn't see. 'This stronghold of Carlos's would be a hard place for a fella to get in uninvited like, Ed,' he said. 'And just as hard to get out of without the chief's blessings,' he muttered.

Ed favoured him with a sour-faced grin. 'You'll see how hard it will be, Yankee, round the next bend in the trail.'

197

The next and last guard post was on a low rocky ridge and manned by three men. Joel gave it more than a cursory glance then let his breath out in a loud gasp. 'Well I'll be damned!' he said. 'The sonsuvbitches have hauled a Gatling gun up there!'

'They sure have,' replied Ed. 'That wicked beauty would cut to pieces any unwanted visitors riding in. It could hold back a whole regiment of horse soldiers until every man in the camp had lit out seeking a safer hole-up.'

The pass opened up into a broad, grassy valley with tents, ramshackle huts, and wickiups on both sides of a clear water creek. The camp was just coming to life, with spark crackling flames of fires being stoked up, women filling containers at the creek, and part-dressed men coming out of their living quarters, yawning, coughing and breaking wind.

'I've stayed in worse places, Ed,' Joel said.

'Me likewise,' Ed replied. 'One time

back there in Missouri I hid out at a critter's cave,' he added reflectively, in what to Joel was a softer-toned voice for the burly outlaw.

As they rode further along the creek, Joel saw several full-blood Indians squatting around a fire passing a whiskey bottle between them. Three of the warriors had women sitting beside them. Drawn-faced, dead-eyed white women. Joel's face stoned over. If Carlos had handed over Mrs Slatts and the young girl to some Indians then they could be on their way to a hell he would have no hope of finding.

'Those red devils are some of Carlos's tradin' pards,' Ed said. 'That big hut over there is his place. He ain't an early riser, especially if he's got himself a new bed warmer.' He gave Joel a direct-eyed look. 'It could be the young girl you're seeking, Yankee. It ain't no good not accepting that likelihood.'

Joel didn't want to think about that fearful possibility. If he did he would kick Carlos's door in and gut shoot the bastard as he lay in his bed and to hell what would happen next. Instead he concentrated on looking at the many camp-fires for any signs of the two women.

'Pull up here, boys,' Ed ordered. 'When we see to the horses you and the kid, Yankee, sit at that fire with my boys. And act friendly like as though you're pleased to be here to any of the bastards who come to have words with you. My boys are known here, but you and the kid ain't and they could be curious about you.' Ed eyed Joel. 'And no matter how worried you are about the fate of those two females, don't go snooping around. I'll do that for you. Remember we're walking on eggs here. Me and Carlos ain't what you would call kissin' cousins. If he reckons I'm no longer worth tradin' with we'll all end up stretched over some ant hill. So don't be caught making any moves that could upset him, OK?'

'I get the message, Ed, you're still the

fella dishin' out the orders,' replied Joel, as Ed dismounted and walked across to the nearest group of *comancheros*.

Joel and Jimmy had seen to their horses and were sitting smoking and drinking coffee with Ed's gang exchanging forked-tongued '*Buenos dias, amigos*' with any *comancheros* who came up to the fire.

'Well we've got ourselves here, pard,' Joel said, casual-voiced, trying to keep Jimmy from thinking what his ma and the girl he was fond of could be suffering. 'Ed will find out if your ma and Miss Kathy are in the camp then it's beholden to us to come up with a plan to get them outa this place without us or them comin' to any harm.'

Jimmy didn't answer him, he just sat gazing unseeing into the fire. He still couldn't think clearly. He was impatient to get on to his feet and do his own searching of the camp for his ma and Miss Kathy. They could be in any of the shacks and tents going through hell and here he was sitting smoking, something he had never done before, as though he was enjoying passing the time of day with the murderous scum who could be doing terrible things to his ma and Miss Kathy. Gradually he began to think straight. Did he really believe he could go storming through the camp blazing away with his Colt until he found his ma and Miss Kathy? Then somehow rustle up a couple of horses? All he had to do next, after holding several score of deadly killers at bay, was to get them past the Gatling gun on the ridge that Megan had said could cut down a whole regiment.

Though it was hard for him to do so, Jimmy accepted it was waiting and praying time that Megan would come back with some good news for him. He took a deep pull on his makings which set him off into a fit of eye-watering coughing that brought grins from the outlaws, causing Jimmy to think that he was still a green kid in their hard-bitten way of life.

Carlos was in a mad-eyed mood as he

got up from his bed, the 'breed girl he had been sleeping with was still asleep. He cursed and grabbed a handful of her long black hair, and dragged her savagely out of bed, screaming with pain and terror.

'*Vaya! Ràpidemente!*' he spat.

He lifted a hand to strike the girl across the face but she dodged the blow and dashed to the door and ran outside, still sobbing, trying to hide her nakedness with her hands.

As he was getting dressed Carlos heaped curses on the head of Red Dog. He had returned to the stronghold to fulfil the lustful thoughts he had racing through his mind regarding the Texan girl, only to have them dashed on seeing the Comanche chief in the camp. Red Dog, if he had seen the girl, would have wanted her for himself. To keep the good trading deals he had going with the Comanche he would have had to give him the smooth-skinned, yellow-haired maiden. Carlos had enough men hunting for him, making an enemy of a powerful Comanche *jefe*, who knew the hidden trails to his stronghold was an enemy too many. He'd had to control his lust. He ordered one of his men to take the *señorita* and *señora* to the nearest empty hut and guard them well. Carlos gave a wolfish grin. If he couldn't get his needs satisfied, neither would Antonio.

'Touch either of them, *mi amigo*,' he said ominously to the guard. 'And you will die slowly and painfully.'

Now when he invited Red Dog into his shack to share a bottle of fine whiskey with him the *jefe* would only see the 'breed girl, his usual woman.

★   ★   ★

Megan came back to the camp and sat down at the fire to look across it at the impatient, nerve-twanging Jimmy. 'Your ma and the girl are here, kid,' he said. Seeing the look on Joel's face, he added, 'They're OK, they haven't been used, yet.'

'Where are they?' Jimmy asked, trying to keep his voice low but halfway on to his feet looking wildly about him.

'Take it easy, kid!' Ed snapped back. 'We don't want to call attention to ourselves. Most of these sonsuvbitches hate gringos' guts. Carlos has them locked up in that shack in front of those trees. The chief of those Injuns over there has a strong fancy for fair-skinned Texas females so Carlos is keepin' her out of his sight until the war band rides out. Leastways that's what the Mex who's guardin' them told me.'

Joel glanced over his shoulder at the hut, taking in the guard squatting at the door and the numerous *comancheros* close by. Not wanting to down the boy's high hopes, he kept his thoughts that it would be one hell of a task to get the women out of the hut without raising the alarm, unspoken. Instead he said, 'How long is it before our red brothers quit the camp, Ed?'

'According to that guard,' replied Ed, 'this Red Dog and his wild boys pay a visit here regularly for a four-day drinking session. That means they should be riding out sometime tomorrow.'

'I did say that time wasn't on me and the kid's side,' Joel said. 'It's sure runnin' tight now. I never expected the women to have been guarded.' He gave Jimmy a hard-eyed stare. 'It's no good us not thinkin' that we've one big problem facin' us, boy. Go at it wild-assed could get us both dead, then we'd sure be no help to your ma and the girl.'

Jimmy didn't answer him. He was realizing that being a man he had to face problems' like a man. Boyish wishes and hopes that somehow he could rescue his ma and Miss Kathy didn't work. He would have to rely on the experts, Mr Garretson and the outlaw Ed Megan, to come up with a solution.

Ed grinned at Joel's gloomy-faced look. 'It'll be no sweat getting those females out of that hut, Yankee. The guard will do that for us. When they need to relieve themselves, he escorts them to a patch of brush at the rear of the hut. And he can easily be taken care of.' He looked at Jimmy. 'No disrespect to you, or your ma, but that guard is all eyes while the ladies are doing what they need to do.'

'If Carlos doesn't want that Injun chief seein' the girl,' Joel said, 'the guard won't let the women out until it's dark.' He shot a fleeting humourless smile at Megan. 'And here's me thinkin' that once I had shaken the dust of the high country off me my throat-slittin' days would be over.'

'Me and the boys have found that life isn't what you hoped it would be,' replied a sombre-faced Megan.

'What I'm hopin' right now,' Joel said, 'is for that guard not to be missed for at least a coupla hours. I'll need that much time for us to sneak past those lookouts with the Gatling gun. And the other guards we spotted ridin' in. But, though I'm a pilgrim who always looks on the bright side, I can't see me gettin' that luck.'

Joel fell silent, head down, gazing into the fire for a while as he contemplated the hazardous task he was about to take on. If it had only been his life at stake he would have hightailed it out of the camp, lying low on Crowbait, Indian style, and taken the chance that speed and darkness would see him through unharmed. Three lives, two of them female, was a heavy burden to bear. Though a clean death by the bullet would be more merciful for Mrs Slatts and the girl than what waited for them in Carlos's hands. Finally he raised his head and looked at Ed.

'But that's my problem, Ed,' he said. 'You'll have your mind occupied with how you're goin' to put paid to Carlos.'

'Yankee, you know how the boys feel about Carlos having his way with those Texan women,' Ed said with some heat in his voice. 'We'll back your play to get those females outa this hellhole. We'll give you all the time you need to pussy-foot around those guards.' Ed grinned. 'Leastways Milt will. He's ugly enough to pass himself off as a Mex in the dark squattin' outside that shack door. Stick a Mex hat and a poncho on him even Carlos won't know he ain't the genuine article at a distance.'

Joel mirrored Ed's grin. 'If I can't swing by those bastards unseen it won't be your fault. But how are you goin' to kill Carlos, just outa curiosity so to speak?'

'Come first light,' replied Ed. 'I intend strollin' into his shack and knifing the sonuvabitch while he's still sweet-dreaming.' He grinned at Joel. 'M'be not as slick as you, Yankee, but he'll be just as dead. Then me and the boys will ride out, nice and easy, waving our goodbyes to our amigos up on the ridge.'

Ed's smile slipped as he glanced over Joel's shoulder. 'And speaking of the devil, here comes the bastard now. Now don't any of you boys give Carlos an unkind look, remember we're here to help the Yankee rescue those two Texan ladies.'

Joel looked over his shoulder and saw the short, thickset Mexican coming towards them. He noted that although Carlos was in his stronghold, surrounded by his men, he was well armed, with two heavy calibre pistols belted about his pot-belly and a machete dangling on a loop at his right side. Carlos, he opined, was a real careful man. As he came nearer, Joel got a closer look at Carlos's face. He believed that a man's character showed through his face and by what he could see in the cruel, snake-eyed visage, Carlos was long overdue for planting. Sitting Bull, Gall, Crazy Horse, and Red Cloud, noted white-eye killers had more pleasant-looking faces.

'And that weasel-faced fella following him,' he heard Ed say softly, 'is Antonio, Carlos's sidekick. He isn't what you'd call a fine figure of a man, but when it comes to killing he runs a close second to his boss.'

Carlos, though smiling, subjected Joel and Jimmy to a cold-eyed calculating look. Joel hoped that Jimmy wouldn't let the anger he held against the chief from showing or they both would be dead. As he had already assessed, Carlos was one careful man. If he so much as sensed that the gringos he hadn't seen before were a threat to him his pistols would clear leather and deal out quick death.

'Did you get much *dinero* in Texas, Señor Megan?' Carlos asked.

'It ain't any use saying otherwise, Carlos, things went badly wrong for us in Texas,' Ed said. 'We got no riches and I lost some good men.' He nodded to Joel and Jimmy. 'They're two new members of the gang. I hope to build it back to full strength again.' Ed didn't mention to Carlos that he knew of his Texas raid, thinking as long as the chief felt he had put one over the gringo *bandidos* he would be in a welcoming mood.

He was proved right when Carlos said, 'You and your men can stay in my camp, Señor Megan. M'be later we will discuss setting up our trade deal again.'

Again Joel felt the *comanchero* chief's suspicious-eyed gaze sweep over him and the kid before he and Antonio moved on to the Indians' camp-fire. 'I've killed during the war and when I was a scout for General Miles, Ed,' he said. 'But only when it had to be done. I've never really had a cold blood urge to kill, not till I saw your amigo, Carlos.'

Ed grinned fiercley. 'Don't put your urges into action, Yankee, that sonuvabitch is mine. Now let's all rest up for a spell, and that means you, kid, as well. A tired man is no good to his pard if things go wrong.' He cast a sweeping glance at what was left of his gang. 'And you boys lay off the tequila, OK? A drunken man is more useless than a tired one in a shoot-out. We have to be prepared for the worst come dark. Isn't that so, Yankee?'

'I couldn't put it better myself, Ed,' replied Joel. 'Luck's been with us so far but we'd be foolish not to think it could suddenly go against us.'

15

It was a trembling with part fear, part excitement Jimmy who held Crowbait and his horse's reins on the far edge of the patch of brush. Somewhere, out there in the dark, on the other side of the undergrowth, Mr Garretson was waiting to kill quickly and quietly the man who was guarding his ma and Miss Kathy.

Just before it was time to make their moves, Jimmy had asked Joel why there were only two horses when four of them would be riding out.

'It's a risky enterprise we're about to embark on, boy,' Mr Garretson had replied. 'We don't want to add extra risk by sneakin' along to the horse lines and trying to lift a coupla horses and saddle gear. But supposin' that came easy, it would mean four sets of iron-shod hoofs for the guards with the rapid-firing gun to hear passin' below them. And your ma and the girl won't be in a fit state to be able to lead a horse silently over that rough trail. Crowbait can step lightly when he has to, but I ain't sure about your mount so find some cloth, old clothes, whatever, to muffle its feet with.

And Jimmy was left with the thought that he had a lot yet to learn to stay alive in an owlhoot's world where a wrong move could bring death.

Joel took a firm grip on the stone hatchet he had picked up at the Indians' camp. He couldn't chance using his knife in the dark, a fumbled thrust and the guard would have time to call out before dying. A blow on the head with the hatchet would silence him quickly and forever. All was set for the rescue. The kid was waiting with the horses and seemingly steady-nerved enough for the job ahead and Milt wearing his Mex gear ready to take over as the guard. An extra, unexpected, but welcome promise from Ed Megan that if things went wrong, he and his boys would help him shoot his way out of the camp made Joel, in no ways an emotional man, reach out and shake Ed's hand with a muttered, 'Much appreciated, pard.'

Joel saw the yellow glow of light as the rear door of the shack opened. He caught a glimpse of the women stepping out into the night followed closely by the guard carrying a lantern. He stiffened up, the killing time was here. Hc let the trio pass him, then followed them as light-footed as an Indian stalking a white-eye scalp.

Mrs Slatts held Kathy's hand, squeezing it to comfort her. She had seen the leering grin the guard had given them when she had asked him if they could go outside and though she prided herself on being a devout Christian she would not hesitate to shoot the man dead if the opportunity came for putting her and Kathy through this humiliating, degrading experience. And she firmly believed that God would forgive her for doing so.

When they reached the edge of the bush, she whispered to Kathy, 'Run deeper in, girl, it's thick enough to hide from the filthy scum to get a few minutes to ourselves.' Both of them dashed into the undergrowth heedless of the sharp branches slashing their bare arms and faces. Mrs Slatts managing a brief smile as she heard the guard stumbling and cursing behind them, his lantern bobbing wildly in the air.

Joel stepped in close, a great ominous shadow dwarfing the much smaller Mexican. He brought the hatchet sweeping down with much hate in his heart. The sickening crack of a crushed skull gave him much satisfaction. Like a burst feed sack the guard sank to the ground without so much as a dying groan. Joel managed to grab hold of the lantern before it hit the grass and started a fire.

Mrs Slatts saw the lantern coming

towards them. At least you haven't had your perverted treat this time, she thought. She took hold of Kathy's hand again to wait for the guard's tirade at them for running away. Instead she heard, 'It's OK, Mrs Slatts, it's me, Mr Garretson.' It was a voice she had given up hope of ever hearing again. Then there Mr Garretson was, standing in front of her, tall, resolute-faced, holding a hatchet in his other hand. He had killed yet again to protect the Slatts family.

'How did you . . . ' she sobbed, tears filling her eyes as she clutched Kathy tightly to her.

'There ain't no time for explanations, ma'am,' replied Joel. 'We've got to get outa here, fast. Jimmy's on the other side with the horses.'

'Jimmy's here?' Mrs Slatts gasped

'You'll be surprised who's here helpin' you to escape,' Joel said. 'Now let's get movin', ladies, before the boy gets restless and comes to seek you out.'

Ed, keeping a watchful eye on the

guard, saw him go into the shack. He waited for several minutes and not hearing any shouts of alarm or firing behind the shack, guessed that the tall Yankee had disposed of the guard and that things were going as planned. He gave the nod to Milt to go and put on his act.

Ed looked at his gang sitting at the fire, drawing on their cigarillos, rifles resting easy across their knees. All of them, including himself, were as strained-faced as if they were about to step in some bank and demand the contents of its safe. Though in spite of that, Ed was experiencing an unusually good feeling that he was doing the right thing helping the tall Yankee rescue the Texan women even if it meant a bloody shoot-out with Carlos and his small army of cutthroats. Ed's lips twisted in a semblance of a smile. He had to go a long way back in his memory to remember doing anything good for anyone but the Ed Megan gang.

The moon was full in a cloudless sky, the bluffs and ridges lining the pass casting deep long shadows. Under the dark blanket, Joel led his small party out of the stronghold, the females up on the horses. They had skirted along the edge of the camp, the four of them on foot then, keeping a line of trees between them and the camp-fires.

Before they had reached the ridge where the Gatling gun was positioned Joel gave out his first order. 'If the alarm is raised, boy,' he said, 'you leap up alongside the girl and get to hell outa here with her and your ma, savvy? I want none of this hogwash from you about wantin' to stand by your pard; your pard is old enough to lookout for himself. We have come here to rescue your ma and the girl and that's all that matters.'

One look at his partner's bone-hard face deterred Jimmy from questioning his order. 'I'll do that, Mr Garretson,' he said, admitting to himself that Mr Garretson was right, his ma and Miss

Kathy's lives did come first.

Joel kept his gaze on the outpost catching sight of several huddled figures crouched over a small fire. He gave a grunt of satisfaction. He was banking on the guards, confident that their stronghold was well hidden, being asleep, or at least not fully alert. That did not stop Joel from feeling that he was ageing fast with every step he took, figuring he would be white-haired before they got in the clear and out on the open plain. He could have stayed in Montana and let the Sioux and the Crow turn his hair prematurely grey. Though, then again, staying up there in the high country would have meant he would never have met up with the sweet-smiling Widow Slatts, a female worth a few grey hairs.

Joel tugged lightly at Crowbait's reins. 'Now you keep steppin' lightly, old friend,' he said. 'Or me and the boy and those two fine ladies will be in deep trouble. But if it comes, you hightail it outa here with the boy. Don't act stubborn and hang back with me.'

Joel felt rather than heard a ripple of a growl in Crowbait's throat and guessed that the horse had got his message. Or it had just been wind and he was going loco with worrying about the two women.

Mrs Slatts had heard Mr Garretson muttering but could not make out what he was saying. What he was attempting to do would cause an archangel to mutter to himself. Her heart went out to him. She wondered if Mr Garretson had left a wife in Montana and would ask her to come to Texas once his place was ready for her. If he wasn't married she would willingly offer to be his wife. She knew she wasn't a beautiful-looking woman but she could cook and sew and keep a clean house for a man. Then the middle-aged Widow Slatts wondered whether or not being a captive of the comancheros had addled her brain thinking such wild thoughts when not a half a mile behind them was a campful of savage killers who could at any moment discover they had gone and come howling after them. And a good man, whom she hardly knew, who had come to Texas to escape the dangers and killings in Montana, would die alongside her. It would be all her fault. The Widow Slatts sobbed, silently but profusely.

Jimmy was going through his own lonely hell of fear and apprehension, though he was trying hard to walk tall alongside his horse. Miss Kathy had kissed him and given him a brief hug when she and his ma had come running out of the brush. That sweet moment had long gone, washed away by the sweat of fear soaking his shirt. Every now and again as he drew back his horse to negotiate a tricky stretch of shale-covered trail Kathy's left leg brushed against his shoulder. He felt it shiver and twitch. His fear was nothing compared with what she must be suffering. Jimmy began to walk with a genuine, bolder stride.

Kathy told herself that she was the

granddaughter of a plainsman, an Indian fighter, who had carved a grand cattle ranch from out of a wild land, peopled by equally wild inhabitants, brown and white skinned. She owed not only to her pride but more importantly to Mr Garretson and Marshal Slatts who were putting their lives on the line for her, not to act like a city girl lost on the Great Plains on hearing the howls of the wolves and coyotes. She tried hard to control her fears.

Jimmy heard a hoarse whispered, 'Hold it there, boy,' from Mr Garretson. He pulled his horse to a halt.

'Megan told us that the trail out always bore to the right,' Joel continued. 'And that presents us with one helluva problem. As you can see the trail splits here. To take the right fork will mean us steppin' out across ground lit up as clear as daylight. And I've got a gut-feelin' that up there behind us is at least a coupla lookouts.' He favoured Jimmy with one of his chilling smiles as he drew out the hatchet from his belt.

'I'll sneak up there to see if my hunch is right. If you hear any shootin' it won't be me doin' it, so you get those ladies outa here. If I'm OK I'll make it out on foot. High country is high country, my territory. There ain't no *comanchero* sharp-eyed enough to track me up on those ridges.'

Jimmy's fears came flooding back. He was the man in charge, the *hombre*. Yet Mr Garretson trusted him to lead his charges to safety. All he had to do was prove Mr Garretson's faith in him. And by heck, he thought he would prove him right. Jimmy's face tightened with resolve until it was as grim-looking as his partner.

Joel smelt tobacco smoke before the crest levelled out and he saw the two guards, backs to him, sitting at the fire. The way to the ridge was steep and his progress hadn't been as fast as he had wanted. Time had been the pressing need since they had first mounted up to try and rescue the women. No more so than now when at any moment the alarm could be raised in the camp, then Carlos with his hell riders would come storming along this pass to regain his Texan prizes.

The last few feet of ground between him and his still unsuspecting victims had to be crossed with speed not stealth. In a mad dash, long coat flapping like the wings of some gigantic night bird of prey Joel cleared the ground in a matter of seconds. His surprise was complete. The two *comancheros* barely had time to turn round and face their danger, no time at all to make a grab for their rifles before the flailing hatchet did its deadly work. The blade sliced deep into the neck of one, drawing out a dark fountain of his life-giving blood. As he slipped sideways, Joel's back-hand-sweeping blow crushed the skull of his *compañero*, the fierceness of the blow lifting him inches off the ground to fall across the fire.

Then Joel was part running, part ass-sliding back down to the floor of the pass, only to hear a sound that froze the sweat on his body, gunfire from the *comancheros'* camp. He dropped to the ground alongside Jimmy, bending low and resting his hands on his knees to calm down his breathing. 'You heard it, boy,' he panted. 'Ed and his boys seem to be in trouble.' Straightening up he said, 'So get the women outa here before that trouble comes this way.'

'What are you going to do, Mr Garretson?' It was a worried-looking Widow Slatts who spoke.

Joel gave her a lopsided grin. 'I don't rightly know, ma'am, except to try win some time for you to get clear of this place. Now git, and keep your eyes skinned, boy, there could more lookouts ahead of you. I'll catch up with you all later.'

Joel watched them ride across the moonlit stretch of the trail then disappear into the darkness behind the butte that had split the trail, thinking that the kid would do all right. Whether he would do likewise he was soon to find out. He set off, armed now with his rifle, in a loping, ground-eating run back along the trail.

By the sound of it Megan and his boys were keeping their promise but they couldn't hold off the opposition for long. Joel was hoping to get his hands on the Gatling gun then by hell, he thought, Carlos would know he had a war on his hands, and not running in his favour.

The pass began to broaden and Jimmy hoped they had safely passed the last of the guards. He could feel the warmth of Miss Kathy's body on his back and her head resting lightly on his right shoulder with her arms about his waist. Although he was feeling physically bushed he felt great. Soon she and his ma's terrible ordeal would be over. He reckoned he had stood fair and square alongside such hard men as Mr Garretson and Ed Megan and his wild boys.

A shadow of a figure coming out of the deeper darkness to his left almost caught him off guard. With a speed that surprised him his pistol was in his hands, cocked and fired. Its flash lit up a pock-marked snarling face then the *comanchero* fell back into darkness. Kathy screamed and tightened her hold on him.

'Give Crowbait his head, Ma!' he yelled, digging his heels hard into his horse's flanks. Chancing a wildly aimed shot in the dark was a lesser risk than being jumped by a *comanchero*. With Kathy clinging to him, pistol still fisted and Crowbait keeping pace, they sped along the last of the defiles.

★ ★ ★

Ed Megan cursed as a shot tore splinters off the window frame close by his head. He fired back at one of the many gun flashes ringing the shack and believed he heard a cry of pain. He knew that the only reason why Carlos had not ordered his men to swamp them with gunfire, or rush them, was that he didn't want to risk killing the

Texan girl. As long as Carlos thought she was in the shack the more time it would give the Yankee to get her and the older woman well clear of the stronghold. Ed didn't doubt that the chief would become impatient and storm the shack. As long as he took Carlos to hell with him every god-damned *comanchero* in the camp could come at them.

He had been sitting at the fire counting off the minutes since the big Yankee and his party had sneaked out of the camp. He reckoned they should be past the main guard with the Gatling though there still was a lot of dangerous ground to cover before they would be well clear of the camp. Then the son-of-a-bitch Antonio put the Yankee's chance of getting the women out of Carlos's clutches in jeopardy.

The horny dog must have been lusting after the older woman and had gone over to the shack to get her. Milt had no choice but to shoot Antonio once the *comanchero* had seen that he was not the proper guard. A single shot in the camp would have raised no alarm, putting it down as some drunken *comanchero* or Indian having a shot at the moon. But the hair-raising, high-pitched scream of a man dying hard from a belly wound would raise the Devil himself. It raised scores of rifle-armed devils.

Like disturbed ants, yelling men ran about the camp, some to where Antonio lay with his heels drumming the ground in his last painful dying spasms, his screams now only a pitiful gurgle of sound. The Megan gang sprang to their feet, looking at each other, hesitant in what they should do to save their necks.

'Fort up in the shack, boys,' Ed called out. 'These bastards are nervy enough to cut loose at their own shadows and we could catch some of their wild fire. When Carlos finds out it was one of us gringos who shot his best pal, they'll shoot at us in earnest.'

They cleared a way to the shack with a rapid burst of gunfire, killing or scattering the *comancheros* standing over the now dead Antonio.

And here they were, Ed thought, boxed in as Pat had said, as tight as Santa Anna encircled Colonel Travis's men at the Alamo. But the colonel had been ordered to fight to the last man. Once the clouds covered the moon they would sneak out of the shack then make it to their horses. It wasn't the first time Ed had led his men, belly on the ground, then through a line of Pinkertons and marshals who thought they had the Megan gang hemmed in.

Joel, heaving and panting like a run-into-the-ground horse, came over the lip of the Gatling gun ridge, a post manned by three men, who, to Joel's advantage, were gazing down at the commotion in the camp. He walked slowly towards them firing his rifle from the hip at every step he took. The fusillade sent two of them tumbling over the rim, the third guard managed to swing round and pull off a wild shot at Joel with his pistol that drew blood on Joel's right arm before he pumped two shells into his chest. The *comanchero* staggered back several paces until he was treading on air then followed his *compadres* in rolling down the side of the ridge, dead long before he hit the floor of the canyon.

Joel looked down at the camp and saw the ring of gun flashes around the shack where the women had been held prisoners. 'Ed Megan,' he breathed, 'some folk may want to see you strung up but takin' as you find, you are a man who stands by his word, and then some. Now, it's about time I repaid some of the debt I owe you.'

He swung the Gatling round until the barrel was pointing down into the camp. There was already a magazine clipped in, all he had to do was to crank the handle.

The sound of the the rattling roar of the gun bounced off the canyon walls and the heavy calibre shells raised a wall of dust in front of the shack. For one depressing moment, Ed thought that Carlos had ordered the rapid-firing gun to put an end to the standoff. Then he heard the screams of wounded men, and men leaping over fires in their efforts to escape the deadly hail. He turned away from the window, grinning. 'That big Yankee is dealing out death by the second to back us up. It's the break we need to get to the horses.'

Carlos hadn't played all his cards. He knew that the gringo *bandidos* were *hombres* of great cunning and would not be so loco as to stay in the cabin until daylight when all hope of escaping would be ended. He and six of his *muchachos* were waiting in ambush on the rim of the hollow where the horses were tethered.

Ed, in a crouching run, led his men, unsuspectingly, into a killing field. With a blaze of gunfire, Carlos snapped his trap shut. The four Texans were swept off their feet as though cut down by an invisible scythe, Ed suffered a pain-gasping blow on his left side that dropped him groaning to the ground with a fire burning hot inside him. Milt ate dirt fast, and by some good luck or other, escaped being killed or wounded.

In the slight lull in the firing, he heard Ed ask if he was OK. 'Up till now, I am,' he replied. 'But the Texan boys are all done for. Are you OK?' The firing started up again and he couldn't hear Ed's reply. Flattening himself further into the contours of the ground as shells whizzed their deadly way inches above his cringing body he belly crawled across to Ed.

'We walked into this one like a bunch of green-horns, Ed,' he said. 'That sonuvabitch greaser outfoxed us. He's with the bastard who's shootin' at us. Are we gonna risk goin' for our horses? We'll get plugged for sure if we stay here.'

'I'll never make it, Milt,' Ed said. 'I'm sorely wounded, but I ain't passin' over until I've put paid to Carlos.

'I'll back you up, Ed,' Milt said.

'Like hell you will!' Ed snarled. 'When I make my play you get the hell outa here. I don't want to give that greaser bastard the satisfaction of wipin' out the whole of the Ed Megan gang. Now let's work an Injun trick on him by lyin' low and playing dead. Let him think he's downed all of us.'

Carlos hearing no return fire from the gringos grinned and slowly raised himself from the ground. 'Go down, *muchachos*,' he said, 'and make sure all the gringo dogs are dead.'

Ed saw his bulky silhouette, his high-steepled sombrero. Not without a great deal of pain and mumbled cursing, Ed struggled on to his feet. Lips drawn back in a fearsome grin, the pistols he held flamed and bucked in his hands. For a fleeting moment he was a Missouri brush boy fighting back against great odds. He heard Carlos's dying screams, then the *comancheros* killed him several times over. Milt saw Carlos and Ed go down then made a run for it.

Milt had never crawled so fast in his life. The gunfire had sent the horses rearing and snorting with fear, only their tethering ropes prevented them from spooking. Several quick slashes with his knife freed them and they took off in a high-kicking jostling stampede with Milt clinging on to the underside of his mount and in no time at all was well clear of being shot at.

★ ★ ★

As he was reloading the gun, Joel heard a rattle of loose stones behind him. He whirled round, hand clawing for his pistol, then he saw it was Milt. He grinned. 'I could see that you boys were in a tight spot down there, Milt,' he said. 'So the least I could do was to give you some support.'

'It ain't any use helping us any more, Yankee,' Milt replied. 'You're gazing on the last of the Megan gang.'

Joel's smile slipped. 'The last?' he said with disbelief in his voice.

'Yeah, Ed, the Texans, all dead. That sonuvabitch, Carlos, bushwhacked us when we were going for our horses. Though Ed died with a smile on his face, he killed Carlos before he was gunned down. And I did likewise to Antonio.'

'Well, I ain't bein' paid to wipe out a nest of *comancheros*, Milt,' Joel said. 'So let's get to hell outa these canyons. Though your mount will have to carry double, I loaned Crowbait out.'

★ ★ ★

'There's riders comin' in, boss,' said one of the Slash Y men manning the broken-down wall of a derelict stage way station. Men straightened up and levered shells into their Winchesters as they watched the ribbon of trail dust closing in on them. Kathy moved closer to Jimmy and slipped her hand in his. Jimmy gave it a reassuring squeeze. 'You and my ma will be OK,' he told her. 'Your grandpa has the whole Slash Y crew here, enough rifles to hold off a whole army. But those fellas comin' in will be Mr Garretson and Mr Megan and his men, you'll see.'

The Widow Slatts was praying that one of the riders would be Mr Garretson. She would never forgive herself if he had been killed on her behalf. She waited, all tensed up, until she could identify the riders.

'There's a bunch of men up ahead, Yankee,' Milt said.

They were clear of the mountains, and riding across the flat with no signs of any pursuers. Joel looked over Milt's shoulder and saw at least twenty or so men standing in the ruins of a lone building.

'Well I'll be durned!' Joel exclaimed. 'They're the Slash Y crew, Milt, the young girl's grandpa's crew.' As they rode nearer he vented another gasped, 'Well I'll be durned!' as he saw that the Widow Slatts and Kathy were with them.

'It's the big Yankee and another fella, Mr McDowell,' the Slash Y straw boss said. And then ordered his crew to stand down, but to keep their eyes skinned for signs of any more trail dust.

As Milt drew up his horse Joel came to a quick decision. 'I figure you ain't about to take up robbin' banks again, Milt,' he said.

Milt gave a snorting derisive laugh. 'I've had my bellyful of that line of business, Yankee,' he replied.

'Mr McDowell owns the Slash Y and he's here with his boys,' Joel said. 'I reckon he'll only be too glad to offer a man who helped to get his granddaughter from out of the *comancheros*' hands a job on his spread.'

Milt grinned. 'Tending cows is a ball-achin' chore but at least the critters ain't shootin' back at you. I'll take what that rancher offers me, Yankee.'

Mrs Slatts breathed a silent thankful prayer. As Mr Garretson dismounted, she got a clearer look at him and her eyes filled with tears of compassion. He looked like death and he had been wounded in his right arm. She wanted to dash over and embrace him to show her feelings for him, but didn't think it was the right thing a widow should do in front of men she didn't know.

Rancher McDowell came to greet them. Though haggard-faced with sleepless nights and long hours of searching in vain for the *comancheros'* camp his eyes were still alert. 'We were expecting a few more of you coming out, Mr Garretson,' he said. 'According to young Marshal Slatts, when he came fire-ballin' into us, there was a bunch of fellas involved in the rescue. Plus m'be a howlin' mob of *comancheros* chasin' you. That's why we forted up here, making it a strong point for you to bolt to if hard pressed. I wanted to send the ladies back to the Slash Y with an escort but the pair of them insisted that they stay here. Told me that the escort would be needed if the *comancheros* came out of the mountains close on your heels.' The rancher smiled at Joel. 'Mrs Slatts is more than a mite worried about you,

Mr Garretson. And I've got to thank you again for saving my granddaughter's life.'

'This time you have to thank Milt, here,' replied Joel. 'Without him and his buddies' help, me and the boy couldn't have pulled off the rescue. Unfortunately all of them, bar Milt, were killed in the attempt but not before they sent Carlos and his number one man to Hell.' Joel shot a warning, keep-quiet look at Jimmy, but a dreamy-faced Jimmy had lost all interest in the lawless ways of Milt. All he was aware of was that Miss Kathy, although they were in no danger, was still holding his hand, like as if they were walking out together on a regular basis. 'Milt and the rest of the boys,' continued Joel, 'were in New Mexico lookin' for ranch work before they threw their lot in with us.'

Ben McDowell gave Milt a grateful look. 'Milt,' he said. 'You needn't search any more. As from now you're a Slash Y top hand. And I owe you a great deal more than that for getting my grand-daughter out of that hellhole.'

'Bein' on your payroll will do fine, boss,' Milt said. 'Tryin to save the ladies seemed to me and my buddies the natural thing to do.'

The rancher switched his gaze back on to Joel. 'And you, Yankee, get across to that fine-looking widow woman,' he growled good-humouredly. 'And give her a few words of comfort. She's too shy to tell you she's got a lot of good feelings for you.' He grinned. 'And that long streak of misery of a horse of yours needs sweet-talking, too, he's also pining for your company.'

Joel coloured up on hearing the rancher's suggestion before, as smug-faced as his young partner, he walked across to the Widow Slatts, thinking that his long trail from the high country, and all the killing he'd had to do had been worth it.

The smiling Widow Slatts sniffed back her tears and wiped her eyes with the back of her hand. Heedless of what the rough, bawdy-thinking ranch-hands would say when Mr Garretson came up to her, she would throw her arms around him and hold him tight. After all, she thought, it was only right and proper for a woman to hug the man she intended to wed.

THE END

We do hope that you have enjoyed reading this large print book.

Did you know that all of our titles are available for purchase?

We publish a wide range of high quality large print books including:
Romances, Mysteries, Classics
General Fiction
Non Fiction and Westerns

Special interest titles available in large print are:
The Little Oxford Dictionary
Music Book, Song Book
Hymn Book, Service Book

Also available from us courtesy of Oxford University Press:
Young Readers' Dictionary
(large print edition)
Young Readers' Thesaurus
(large print edition)

For further information or a free brochure, please contact us at:
Ulverscroft Large Print Books Ltd.,
The Green, Bradgate Road, Anstey,
Leicester, LE7 7FU, England.
Tel: (00 44) **0116 236 4325**
Fax: (00 44) **0116 234 0205**

WEST OF EDEN

Mike Stall

Marshal Jack Adams was tired of people shooting at him. So when the kid came into town sporting a two-gun rig and out to make his reputation — at Adam's expense — it was time to turn in his star and buy that horse ranch he'd dreamed about in the Eden Valley. It looked peaceful, but the valley was on the verge of a range-war and there was only one man to stop it. So Adams pinned on a star again and started shooting back — with a vengeance!

BAR 10 GUNSMOKE

Boyd Cassidy

As always, Bar 10 rancher Gene Adams responded to a plea for help, taking Johnny Puma and Tomahawk. They headed into Mexico to help their friend Don Miguel Garcia. But they were walking into a trap laid by the outlaw known as Lucifer. When the Bar 10 riders arrived at Garcia's ranch, Johnny was cut down in a hail of bullets. Adams and Tomahawk thunder into action to take on Lucifer and his gang. But will they survive the outlaws' hot lead?

THE FRONTIERSMEN

Elliot Conway

Major Philip Gaunt and his former batman, Naik Alif Khan, veterans of dozens of skirmishes on British India's north-west frontier, are fighting the wild and dangerous land of northern Mexico. Aided by 'Buckskin' Carlson, a newly reformed drunk, they are hunting down Mexican bandidos who murdered the major's sister. But it proves to be a dangerous trail. Death by knife and gun is never far away. Will they finally deliver cold justice to the bandidos?